TRY NOT TO DIE

On

Slashtag

JON COHN

VINCERE
PRESS

Published by Vincere Press
65 Pine Ave., Ste 806
Long Beach, CA 90802

Try Not to Die: On Slashtag
Copyright © 2023 by Jon Cohn

Printed in the United States of America
First Edition

ISBN: 978-1-961740-17-4
Library of Congress Control Number: 2024905821

Front and back cover by Jun Ares
Interior illustrations by Delaney Mamer
Edit by Mark Tullius and Horrorsmith Editing

Welcome to Slashtag!

If you'd like to learn more about the *Slashtag* universe, including an official companion Podcast that follows along with the *Slashtag* novel, visit www.slashtaginsider.com. Yes, it's a real website.

Order autographed books, get cool stickers (seriously, my wife made them), and learn about my latest horror book and board game releases at www.joncohnauthor.com. Also, if you sign up for my newsletter, you'll get a bunch of other cool stuff. I promise!

The story you are about to read is a prequel to Slashtag.

A Note from the Publisher

This *Try Not to Die* is a little different from the others. I reached out to Jon Cohn about the possibility of collaborating after I read *Slashtag*, one of my favorite reads from 2023. Jon, who is also a board game creator, jumped at the idea and got right to work, handing me a complete first draft a few months later. His draft proved that he had all bases covered and all I had to do was come in as an editor along with Lyndsey Smith.

While my ego aches a bit at not being able to take credit for any of the brilliant scenes you're about to experience, I'm incredibly proud of this book. Jon did an amazing job. I hope you're ready for the show and prepared to die again and again.

Mark Tullius

*This book is dedicated to **you**—for being brave, or dumb enough, to step foot into the Propitius Hotel.*
I mean this, from the bottom of my heart:
I hope you die...a lot.

Jon Cohn

MAPS

The Propitius Hotel

— Basement —

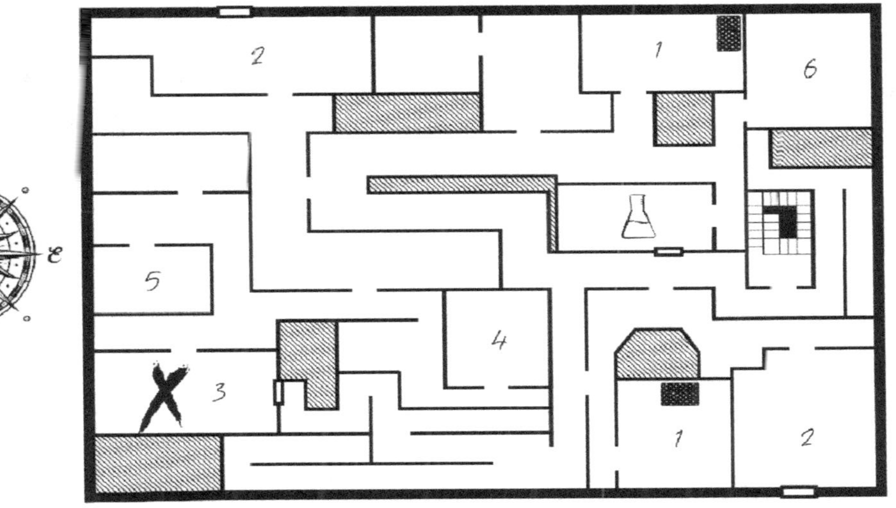

Legend
1. Furnace
2. Distillery
3. Clinic
4. Morgue
5. Storage
6. Electrical

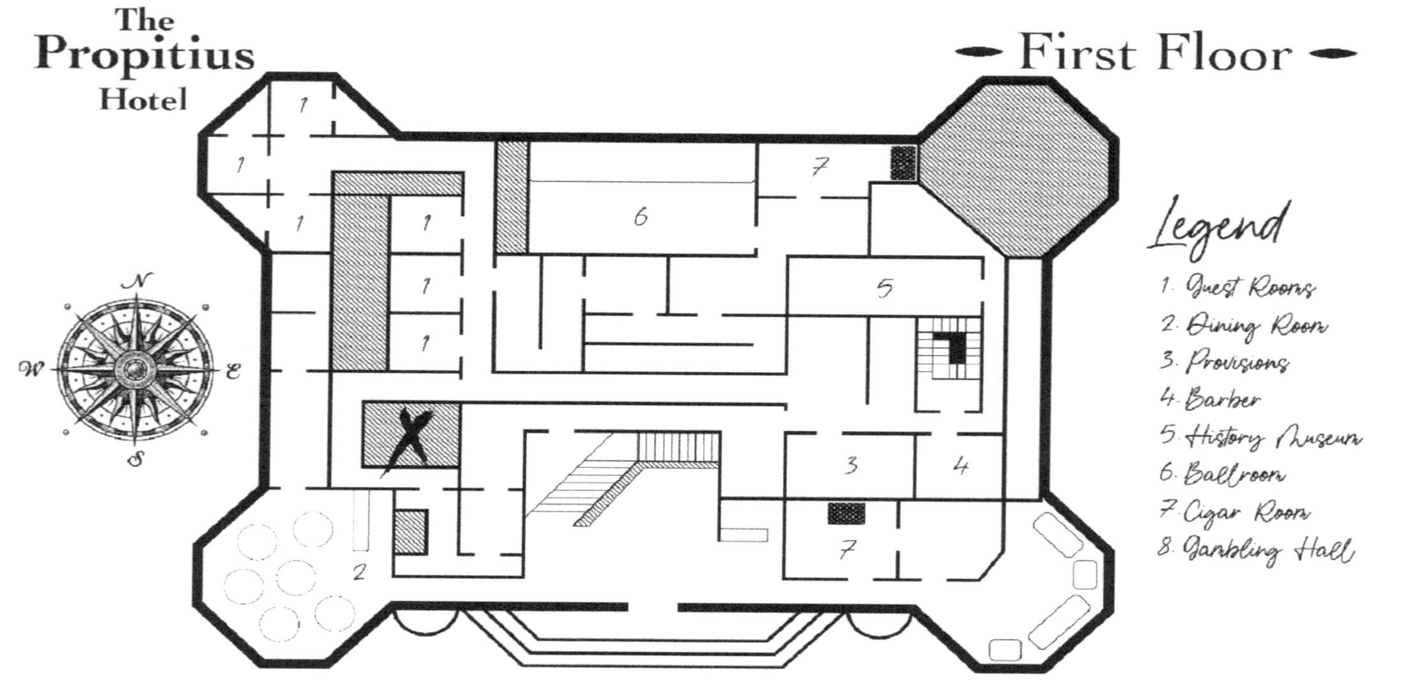

The Propitius Hotel
First Floor
Legend
1. Guest Rooms
2. Dining Room
3. Provisions
4. Barber
5. History Museum
6. Ballroom
7. Cigar Room
8. Gambling Hall
N
E
S
W

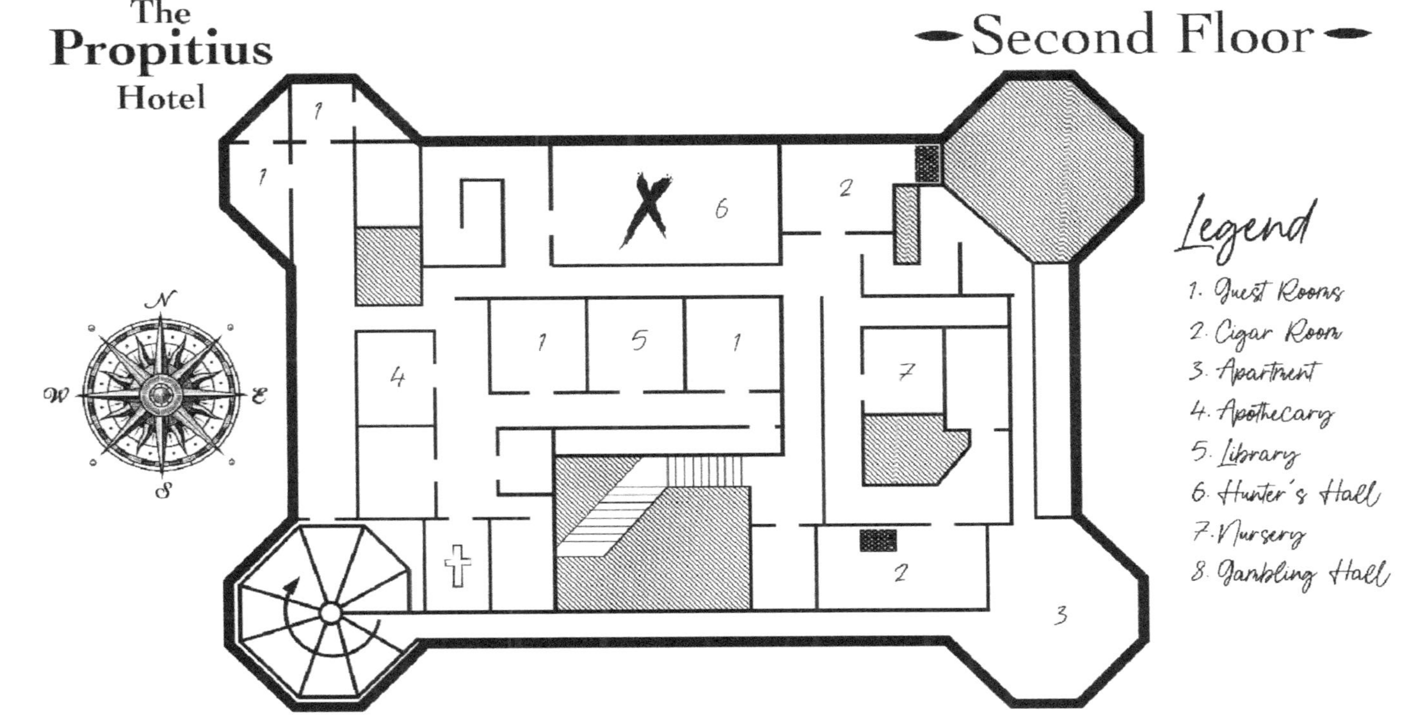

The
Propitius
Hotel
Second Floor
Legend
1. Guest Rooms
2. Cigar Room
3. Apartment
4. Apothecary
5. Library
6. Hunter's Hall
7. Nursery
8. Gambling Hall
N
E
S
W

TRY NOT TO DIE
On Slashtag

In the heart of L.A., there's a sort of competition between studios to see who can push billboard sizes to the absolute limit. The largest you'll find are typically plastered to the backlot walls keeping gawkers from getting into the coveted studios, making sure they tune in on Wednesday nights. Today, I'm not just one of those unwashed masses hoping to make it past that security gate. I *am* the talent.

Well...sort of.

I'm greeted by a thirty-foot mural of reality TV queen Britt Holley, with an even larger KMC Network logo staring down at me, when Chrissy and I pull up to the guard station in her '94 Impala.

The guard leans forward and squints at us, probably not used to seeing such a fine vehicle pass these gates.

"Names and IDs." He checks his clipboard and reaches out his hand expectantly.

"Chrissy Holtz," my driver, and best friend, says, digging through her purse and producing one.

"Jeremy Talbott." I reach across Chrissy to hand him my license.

He studies them for a few seconds, then cross-checks our printed names with a list in his booth.

My pulse pounds. What if there's been a mistake or a miscommunication along the line and our names aren't on the list? There are already several cars behind us—Mercedes and Porsches. How humiliating would it be for us to have to turn around after getting this far?

The guard steps back out and hands Chrissy our licenses. "Welcome to Krentler Media Studios." He uses a highlighter on a paper map, drawing a path for us to park and find their reality TV casting office.

Hollywood, here we are.

"Don't gawk," Chrissy says, exiting the vehicle. "Act like you belong, and you can get anywhere."

She would know. For the last two years at film school, while I've spent almost every waking free hour working on student film sets, Chrissy has been getting non-stop work as an extra on just about every show I can imagine. At this point, I don't even think she remembers her own filmography, and occasionally, I will spot her in the background of some cop drama she has no memory of participating in. Then again, that could also be partially because she's stoned roughly ninety percent of the time.

I follow Chrissy around the studio filled with monolithic and historic yellow buildings, pretending to walk with purpose. She heads straight for the office. We're about to walk in, when a building to my right catches my eye.

"Oh my God," I say, completely starstruck.

Jared Collins, the star of the hit series *Unnatural,* walks past me and through a door of a neighboring building.

"Where are you going?" Chrissy asks when I divert from the path and follow the actor.

*****

Explore the neighboring building. Turn to page 37.
Follow Chrissy. Turn to page 159.

"Fuck me in a forest," Shiv says. "I'm done with this. No more running. If that old crone wants me, she's gonna get more than she bargained for."

Shiv winces, straining to bend over and grab one of the larger shards of crystal in the hand not missing half its digits. She limps behind a large burgundy leather wing chair as quickly as her bleeding leg will allow and holds a blood-soaked crystal shard wrapped in cloth from her sleeve, to protect her hand. Massive stains of black-red are running down the back of her jeans, and she still has her other hand—the fingers severed—shoved into her armpit.

"Find a weapon. She's going to go for PQ's soul first. That's when we strike."

"But Shiv, didn't you say earlier—"

"I don't care what I said before. I'm done. Do you hear me, Jeremy? I'm done with all of this. If I'm dying in here, let me at least go out like gran." Shiv's eyes look feral, like a cornered animal ready to bite whatever hand dares go near her.

Normally in a situation like this, I'd try to give her some space, but she's queueing up for a battle to the death with the Irish version of the Grim Reaper, and I'm worried that, regardless of my actions, I'm about to get dragged into it.

The muffled cries of the Banshee quadruple in intensity when she passes through a wall of books and into the library. Her black dress hangs loosely over her bony frame, with sleeves covering her hands and stark-white hair creating a curtain to obscure her face.

For better or worse, I'm ducked behind the same chair as Shiv. Unlike her, I forgot to grab a makeshift weapon along the way. With no weapon and no understanding of what I'm up against, I have to rely completely on Shiv. An uncontrollable shudder passes through me when I catch a glimpse of the wailing Irish spirit floating toward PQ.

While I'm cowering behind the chair, Shiv breaks her own plan and lunges from our hiding spot, screaming a battle cry. The Banshee stops, cranes her head over to Shiv, and bends slightly to the right, like a dog trying to understand a command. She doesn't react, even when Shiv comes plowing into her, swinging her improvised weapon wildly at the Banshee's face.

Shiv passes through the Banshee as if she were nothing more than a hologram from some science fiction movie. The only difference is, Shiv comes out the other end gasping for breath, choking as she drops her weapon and falls to her knees. The Banshee turns to Shiv, seeming more curious than aggressive. It doesn't stop Shiv from attempting to swing the weapon a few more times, coughing out some incoherent sounds I'm assuming are more swears.

By now, the Banshee is fully invested in watching Shiv's futile attempt at striking back at her childhood nightmare. She bends down, and the sound of Shiv's choking intensifies, so much so she's no longer trying to form words, but instead using all her energy just to pull air into her lungs. From my vantage point, I can't see what's going on.

I leave my hiding spot to get a closer look, broken glass crunching under my shoe. The Banshee whips her head around, her mask of white hair parting just enough for me to see her sunken, pale skin juxtaposed against her glowing red eyes. Behind her, Shiv's face looks almost as twisted and devoid of color as the Banshee's. It's turned an almost-gray color, her eyes rolled back in her head and her body convulsing. The hand with missing fingers falls to her side, and a pool of blood grows, her life force draining from the remnants.

The Banshee floats toward me, and as I instinctually take a step back, more glass crunches under my feet. It seems to invigorate the spirit. Even though her hair is once again a veil over her face, the red of her eyes glows through.

"I-I'm sorry," I say, seeing how Shiv's attack turned out for her and hoping maybe I can somehow talk my way out of sharing her fate.

The Banshee hovers through the table with the crashed chandelier, and somehow, about a half-dozen shards rise from the table on their own, floating around her in orbit. She pulls herself to me, like some sort of bio-magnet.

"Please," I beg, dropping to my knees.

The Banshee stops advancing but continues to cry, giving me hope my act of penitence might get me out of this. The deep, melancholy sobs of the white-haired woman turn into something darker, more malicious—the most hideous laugh I've ever heard.

"I swear I wasn't trying to hurt you," I say, though I know by now it's too late.

She raises her hand in an almost lazy gesture, reminding me of a Victorian duchess presenting her hand to be kissed by a prospective duke. As she does, her dark nightgown's sleeve slides back, revealing a white hand with filthy claws and blackened fingers. With the slightest flick of her wrist, the dozen or so shards orbiting her body all go flying at me like a barrage of arrows, turning me into a human pincushion.

*****

Try again. Turn to page 132.

For a moment, I consider hopping on the table, but the trap doors on either end make me nervous. If I were to lie down, there's no telling which direction I would go once the lever is pulled.

"Maybe the table sunk enough just from Chrissy leaning on it. I don't think anyone needs to *actually* lie on the table." I give the lever a pull to test my theory. A trapdoor opens at the head of the tilting table, confirming exactly how the mechanism works.

"Christ, it's pitch-black down there," Shiv says, peering down the hole. "I don't suppose anyone's got a torch on them? Erm, I mean, a flashlight?"

Just like me, it turns out everyone had all their personal items confiscated back at KMC Studios. Gently, I lower myself into the pit and find a rounded metal path heading downward. It's a slide. I try to squat and walk along it but bonk my head against the rocky ceiling. Letting out a breath, I tell everyone to wish me luck, then lie down and let gravity do the rest. Every few feet, a shockwave arcs across my back, painfully skidding over metal bolts holding the slide together.

As soon as I make out a soft blue down by my feet, I'm hurtled out of the chute, stumbling across a white tile floor. I keep myself upright but can't stop from crashing into a small table full of medical instruments. It's a wonder I don't lose an eye, or slice my hand on the scalpels, saws, hand drills, or any of the other rusted metal implements that could have just as easily been weapons of torture than tools for medicine.

My already frayed nerves have me nearly jumping out of my skin, when a clunking thump causes me to spin around. For his size, PQ doesn't look half as awkward as I imagine I did emerging from the slide. While my momentum kept me skidding across the room, PQ just kind of plops onto the ground. He squints, his eyes acclimating to the light of the room.

"Well, that was a cool way to kick this off. Total *Goonies* vibes."

"Is it safe to slide?" Chrissy asks, her voice a heavily distorted echo.

With half of us already down here, I would hope Chrissy already knows the answer. Then again, I can count on one hand the number of times I've seen her take any form of initiative in school.

"Just go down feetfirst and I'll catch you," I reply.

"There's some pretty vintage stuff in here." PQ picks up a hand drill that's got more crusted brown on it than silver. He gives the hand crank a turn, the boring bit spinning in jagged stops and starts, pushing through decades of rust. "You know they used to use these for all sorts of crazy reasons, lobotomies being the chief purpose, but they also used these to just drill holes in skulls in order to give some extra breathing room for concussed or swollen brains."

"The map showed the morgue in the basement," I say, as indecipherable mumbles echo down the slide. On the far wall, there's a grid of doors I'm assuming were for body storage. In the center of the room, next to where I knocked over the pile of doctor's instruments, sits a table much like the one in the town's clinic, except everything in here is made of steel. While still incredibly vintage, it's a night and day difference from the room we just left.

The words, "Shit or get off the pot," come wafting through the slide in Shiv's brogue, quickly followed by the sound of someone else screaming. I hunker down a little, using strong thighs from carrying heavy film equipment to keep me planted firmly on the ground. Chrissy comes soaring out of the black hole, and I put up my arms to catch her, but my feet slide back along the tile, causing us both to lose our balance and fall to the floor.

"Nice save," Chrissy says, with just a hint of deadpan sarcasm. She pushes herself off me.

From somewhere above, Shiv calls out a warning she's coming down, but I'm distracted by a slick and slightly sticky substance coating my hands. It's on my back too, wetting it as if I'd been sweating in the sun for hours. I rub my fingers together; it's viscous, oily, like...

Oh God.

I bring my fingers to my nose and give them a sniff. "Shiv," I shout into the hole, "you might want to hurry. For some reason, the ground is covered in lighter fluid."

Shiv slides down, her black combat boots wedged on either side to control her descent. "What were you saying?" she asks, casually stepping out from the hole in the wall.

"There's lighter fluid all over the floor." I feel a panic bursting from deep within my core.

"I don't know if this is going to particularly help the situation, but I just tried the door, and it's kind of locked," PQ says.

"You don't think they would..." My words trail off at a rapid clicking sound, which reminds me of the burner on my stove back at my campus apartment. "We have to move!" I let the urgency penetrate my voice. My hope is that I sound more commanding than afraid. Working under pressure is nothing new to me, but I've never experienced anything quite like this.

"Do you think maybe they want us to hide in there?" PQ points to the stacks of body lockers on the far end of the room.

The clicking noise from the upper corner of the room finally stops, and a roaring flame spreads across one wall. It's amazing how quickly the morgue turns from a slightly glistening space to one being overtaken by a blaze of fire.

"Let's do it. Go now!" I shout.

We all sprint away from the fire and toward the lockers. I grab one on the second row from the bottom, press in a switch, and give it a tug. A burst of cool, stale air greets me from within. I glance behind and see the fire has spread to the floor. It's surging toward us, as if it were alive and actively seeking us out. PQ and Shiv are already climbing into their lockers, while Chrissy struggles with hers.

Chrissy's locker pops open, and she screams. "There's a dead guy in here!"

I'm already sitting in my locker and about to slide it closed, but Chrissy's standing there, dumbfounded. I shout for her to open another, but she's frozen in terror.

*****

Shut myself in alone. There's no way to help her now.
Turn to page 109.
Invite Chrissy to share a locker. Turn to page 85.

"I don't think we're going to be solving much of anything with PQ in this state," I say. "It looks like there's an apothecary on the second floor. Maybe we can find some antibiotics or painkillers there." I know PQ is on my side without even needing to check in with him. Shiv's a harder sell, but I'm hoping we can all agree our potential safety should come first.

"Fine. We'll take a quick stop for supplies, then we keep moving," she says with a sharp nod. Shiv gestures over to PQ for me to help carry him up the stairs.

PQ is clearly in agony, though we are able to move him relatively quickly. We each prop him up with an arm around his shoulder. Shiv and I need to focus on his health at the moment, but I'm also looking forward to finding something to help with my own spider bite. It's taking more and more effort per step to not show the growing pain in my ankle.

We make it to the top of the curving stairs and follow a quick left, finding a sign hanging over a door reading: "Apothecary." As is expected by now, Shiv breaks off as soon as we see it and makes a push to be the first one in.

Only the door doesn't budge.

"That's just downright dirty," Shiv says, her nostrils flared. She looks next to the door, at the massive window showing us all the drugs and medicines we're not allowed to have. It's as if the window exists purely to taunt us. Look but don't touch.

"What are you doing?" I ask when Shiv plops onto her rear and starts unlacing a metal-spike-laden boot.

"What do you think? I'm getting us in the damn apothecary. Stand back."

"Is that a good idea?" PQ whispers to me while I carry him a few steps away.

"I think there's only one way to find out," I reply, honestly not having the slightest clue whether some terrible retribution will descend upon us for stepping around whatever intent the house has.

Whether breaking the glass was Krentler Media's intention for us or not becomes irrelevant. Shiv chucks her boot at the window, smashing it into hundreds of tiny shards.

"Watch yourself climbing through," she says, using her other boot to clear off a section of broken window from any spikes of glass.

There's no way PQ is going to make it inside, so I prop him up against a wall and let him slide down to the floor, waiting while Shiv and I search for medicine. I do my best to hop over the area cleared by Shiv without catching any shards of glass, but my ankle nearly sends me falling back when I put pressure on it to vault over the window frame.

"Why can't anything be easy?" Shiv says as I join her by a rack of pill bottles. "I haven't heard of any of this stuff, and most of them don't even have ingredients listed. It's all 'Doctor Wilson's Miracle Muscle reliever,' or 'Wilson and Sons Pain and Fever Panacea.' What the hell's a *panacea*?"

"It's supposed to mean, like, a cure-all, but in all likelihood, it's probably just snake oil." I grab a bottle and read the back. Along with a long list of unpronounceable words, I find one that might just help—acetaminophen. "Then again, this may be the real deal." I carry the glass jar of pills back out into the hallway, shake four out, and split them between me and PQ. "Here, this may help." I do my best to create enough saliva in my mouth to swallow the pills dry.

Despite his condition, PQ seems capable of doing the same.

"All right. We should be feeling better in no time," I say, though as I crouch next to PQ, that overwhelming sense of exhaustion hits me again, and I take a seat beside him.

"How soon before these start to work?" PQ asks, like I could have any possible idea whether or not they even contain actual medicine.

"You should start to feel it soon, I hope. Even if it just relieves the pain—"

My words, my entire train of thought, is violently derailed. A thousand daggers stab at me from inside my stomach. I try my best to hold back a groan of pain, but PQ's moans easily eclipse any sounds I make.

"Oh man, what did you just give me?" PQ asks with a look of shock and betrayal on his face.

I shake my head and speak through gritted teeth. My stomach boils in pure agony. "I don't know. It said, 'pain and fever reducer.'"

"It's not right. Something's not right." PQ starts to cough, dry at first, though he begins making a noise like he's trying to hock up a loogie.

My throat burns. I cough too and feel a strange thickness inside my esophagus. It's almost as if someone just poured a gallon of honey down my throat and the thick, sap-like goo is threatening to seep into my lungs. I clear my throat, attempting to push away the blockage, but all it does is cause the honey to roil inside of me. The more I try to clear it out, the more it burns. Finally, I'm able to cough hard enough that a spray of expectorant spackles my palm. It's almost like little specks of white foam.

I cough again. A deep burning rumble in my stomach lurches all the foaming honey up and out of my mouth. I vomit a huge pile of fizz onto the floor. Doing so only seems to somehow double the already extreme pain I'm feeling inside.

"Hey, Jeremy," PQ says, white foam running down his mouth and chest. "I don't think we should have taken those pills."

*****

The correct answer was to search the library.
Turn to page 74.

I raise my hand, indicating I need to use the little boys' room before we move any further. Even though Lucy extended the invitation, she makes a point of checking the time on her watch after I volunteer.

"Fine. Inside the bank, head to the right of the teller stations."

I hustle across the sand, feeling slightly self-conscious that I'm the only one to take advantage of the bathroom break. To force the old wood open, I lift the door itself while I twist the knob. The line of old teller stations is directly in front of me, with a path leading down either side of the room. I know Lucy said to follow the *right* side, but there's a black electrical wire running from under the front door, across the wood-paneled floor, and heading toward the left side of the building. It must run to some lights, or possibly power some sort of electrical plumbing situation in the bathroom. Assuming Lucy was mistaken when giving me directions, I follow the electrical wire down a hall to the left, through a door.

I immediately realize my mistake.

This isn't the bathroom.

On the far wall sits a bank of monitors, all displaying what appears to be CCTV footage from throughout the hotel. The floor and most of the walls have been lined in white plastic sheeting. On a table in the middle of the room sits a bucket, though its sides are too tall for me to see inside. A fat man with a white lab coat and robust white beard stands over the bucket, with a gold-hilted knife in his hand. He's carving a line across his forearm, letting the blood run from his arm down into the bucket.

My eyes go wide. So do his—he clearly wasn't expecting company.

"Sorry, wrong room." I duck my head in embarrassment and turn to shut the door behind me.

"Wait!" the man calls out, but it's too late.

I'm hurrying across the bank toward the door, wanting to get back to my friends. My hand jiggles the handle, but it won't budge. I try to lift the door, the same way I did before, but it's not working.

"You weren't supposed to see this." The old man with the white beard now stands in the doorway of his makeshift office, with a white towel wrapped around his arm. A red slit of a stain eats its way through the bottom.

"I won't tell anyone." I search past his spectacles and into his eyes for forgiveness. My heart is pounding in my chest, and even though the man is no longer holding a knife, I somehow feel *more* threatened by him.

He nods to me. "I'm sorry, but you've tainted the game. Therefore, you forfeit your right to participate."

Something stirs in the shadows, down the hallway to the right of the cashiers. The direction I should have headed in the first place...

"If it makes you feel better, I'm just as sorry this had to happen as you are. I hate to throw away perfectly good test subjects." The man pulls his glasses off his round face and looks down, cleaning the lenses with the bottom lip of his shirt.

Somewhere above my head comes what sounds like a gas leak at first, except it's happening in small bursts. It's dark in the rafters of the bank, but if I squint hard enough, I can see movement sliding between ceiling beams.

"I know it's not what you're really afraid of, but I suppose it will have to do." The old man shakes his head in disappointment.

The thing in the rafters moves again, and I catch glimpses of yellow and white streak across several beams.

Of course, I realize, the obvious smacking me all at once. It's a snake, just like I wrote on my questionnaire of things I was afraid of. At least, when I wrote it down, I didn't *think* I was scared of snakes.

"All right, jokes over." My voice shakes more than expected. When I answered that I was afraid of snakes, I thought maybe I'd see a two-foot-long garden snake or, at worst, a de-fanged rattlesnake.

Instead, my eyes slowly adjust to the room, discovering a python at least twenty feet in length is slithering toward me from above. Its body is as thick as my thigh, and I have no doubts this thing doesn't even need venom to squeeze the life out of someone my size.

I search the room for somewhere to run. The snake lowers its head and flicks its forked tongue in my direction. I don't know much about snakes, aside from the lesson my mother taught me: the worst thing you can do when confronted by a dangerous snake is run. Instead, I slowly retreat until my back presses up against the front door of the building. Without turning around, I let my hand wander until it finds the handle, then give it a pull.

Nothing happens.

The door seems to be jammed in place, even though I redouble my efforts. The huge python continues to sink from the rafters.

I pull up and back as hard as I can, and the door slides open a couple of inches. If I give it another tug, I might get it cracked open enough to slide through. I plant my legs hard into the ground, preparing to give the door another hard tug with all my might. Just as I shift my weight onto my heels, the yellow python snaps forward, sinking dozens of tiny teeth into my shoulder. They aren't sharp so much as the reptile's jaw is powerful. In a quick motion, it rips me away from the door, spinning my body violently into its own, as if it were made of string and I were a yo-yo being pulled back up by an invisible hand.

Next thing I know, it's got my arms pinned to my side, continuing to wrap itself around me, squeezing tighter and tighter with each rotation. An incredible pressure overcomes me, so powerful it forces all the air out of my lungs, then pops a few of my ribs. My feet leave the ground, my head grows light, and the room starts to spin. I press my arms away from my torso as hard as I can to create a gap for me to take a breath. Either I'm too weak, or it's too strong. Probably both.

The snake squeezes me even harder. The bones in my biceps shatter against the python's strength, and the combination of the extreme pain and lack of oxygen causes the whole world to fade to black.

*****

The correct answer was to head to the clinic.
Turn to page 42.

"I got this one." I round the table, trying to visually measure the distance between the edge of the wood and the book. It's almost the same from each direction, to the point where I don't think it's going to make much of a difference which angle I come from. No matter what I do, I'm going to be splaying my entire body across the table in order to reach this book. At this point, it's not so much a question of *if* I'm going to get stabbed, but rather how *much* I'm going to get stabbed.

I pull my hood over my head, as if it's going to do anything to protect me this time. Just as I'm about to dive onto the table, Shiv calls out to me.

"Wait! What about these extra books?" She holds up the two other books I knocked off the table during my last stunt.

An idea starts to form in my head.

"That's perfect. I've got it. Hand me the books." Shiv does so, and I tuck them into the crook of my damaged arm, avoiding the cuts. I grab one with my good hand and take aim. Only two chances to throw my book at the one on the table. If I'm lucky, I can make its retrieval a bit easier. Or just maybe, I'll manage to knock it off the table altogether.

I crank my arm back and do a couple of practice throws. Even though I'm using my off-hand, thanks to my recent injury, I'm getting a good feeling for the book. When I'm ready, I throw it overhand at *The Ripper*, then feel like a fool when the book opens itself up while spinning through the air. With all the pages splayed out, the book completely diverts its course. It doesn't even come close to touching *The Ripper*.

"Okay, frisbee style," I say, changing my approach for the second throw.

This time, the book remains intact during its flight. However, it only knocks *The Ripper* a few inches, making it barely any easier for me to reach it. My heart sinks.

"Fine. Looks like it's the old-fashioned way." I take a few steps back from the table, prepared for a running start. Charging it, I use the fist of my injured hand to vault me up and outstretch my good arm to reach the book. My fingers connect. I have the book in my grasp.

A shard falls and stabs into my shoulder, making it incredibly painful to pull my arm back. Dozens of shards impact the table, and more pierce me.

But then something curious happens.

I feel no pain at all, just a massive pressure, like something pushed its way through my ear and into my brain. My eyes blink by themselves, and my body stops responding to my commands. Shiv's shrieks sound distant, and warm red runs down my face, blurring my vision as it seeps into my eyes.

*****

The correct answer was to let Shiv decide. Turn to page 128.

There's little good I can do to stop Arthur from killing us both in his current state, so as soon as I reach the landing, I dive for the spectacles. My hand smacks into them, shoving them off the edge harder than I intended. My heart sinks when they fall in slow motion and miss the box by at least a foot.

"Oh Christ," Shiv says behind me.

I turn to her just as Arthur's blade buries itself in Shiv's face, tearing through skin, muscle, and into bone. Her eye is gone, forming a crater in the gorge now splitting her face into hemispheres. She tries to say something, but the blade's holding her jaw in place, so all she can do is grunt. Her remaining eyelid flutters, then goes still in a fully open position.

Arthur rips the saw out of Shiv's face, and she falls to the floor. I scramble to get up, but there's no time, so I grab the wooden chair leg Shiv dropped and swing it like a sword to block Wilson's attack.

The clash of our weapons is nothing like I hoped it would be. The teeth of his saw bite into the chair leg and rip it away from me. I grab onto one of the wooden beams holding the railing of the staircase and yank at it, trying to find some other way of defending myself.

Arthur drops his saw and opts for the wooden leg. I'm tugging as hard as I can at the railing's bars, but there's no give. Helplessly, I watch Arthur lift his new weapon like a knife, then swing, aiming the spiked end of the chair leg for my face.

*****

The correct answer was to save Shiv. Turn to page 100.

We retrace our steps to the mirror that spooked me earlier. It stands nearly six feet tall, with an intricate gold-laced frame. I can't find anything special about it, or anything in the surrounding area. There are some lights on wall sconces nearby, a small side table with a vase, and a few paintings hanging on the wall, and then further back are the door to the basement and the barber shop.

It's hard not to feel at least a little deflated, the three of us somberly surveying our surroundings. We find nothing so obvious as a book in a protective case or really any sort of elements leading us to believe this could be the location of a puzzle.

"I guess let's try taking the mirror down first? Maybe there's another clue behind it," PQ suggests after a long and disappointed silence. He grabs hold of the tarnished gold frame and tries to lift it off the wall. "Whoa. Guys, I take it back. I think we actually might be in the right place after all. The mirror doesn't move. I think there's a hinge along the side here."

"Hmm." Shiv eyes the area once more. "Let's try some of the paintings on the walls, see if they come off."

Shiv grabs a painting of a woman lying luxuriously on a red velvet sofa, while I easily remove a painting of a ship at sea from the wall. As far as I can tell, there's nothing but wallpaper behind them.

"What was the hint again?" I ask, already forgetting the second half.

"'In order for you to find the light, look for yourself in the dead of night,'" PQ recites.

"So...what? We have to come back when it's dark out?" Shiv says. "What the hell are we supposed to do until then?"

I shake my head. "I don't think they mean it literally. What if it just has to be dark in here, meaning the actual hallway?" I head over to the nearest wall sconce and lightly tap against the bulb to check for heat. One thing you learn early on film sets is light bulbs can get extremely hot surprisingly quickly. Without proper protection, it's easy to burn your fingers.

I scrunch my hand into the sleeve of my jacket, then carefully unscrew the bulb. There is still heat against my fingers, but with a cotton barrier, it's cool enough I can touch it without giving myself blisters. It only takes a few twists for the bulb to wink out.

"Great plan," Shiv says when nothing happens.

"Hang on. It probably takes more than one." I repeat the process on two, three, four other sconces. With each turn, I feel just slightly more stupid. It's not until I unscrew the fifth bulb that something happens.

Behind the wall comes the sound of clicks, getting my heart pounding with excitement. The mirror creaks, and its huge frame swings out, revealing a passage into a pitch-black room.

"Well, wouldja look at that. You did it, buddy!" PQ says, patting me on the back.

I have to admit, the feeling of accomplishment briefly eclipses the constant fear for my life, and I'm able to appreciate, once again, being a valued member of the team.

"Great. You got us one step closer to our untimely death," Shiv says. "What do you want, a parade? Let's keep moving." She takes the lead, stepping into the black hallway and peering down both directions.

"There's a staircase to the left and a light at the top."

"That must be the light the riddle talks about," I say, still trying to ride high on my win.

Shiv stalks up the stairs and walks through the door at the top, with as much caution as she would give to entering her apartment. "Well, this is *just* grand. What are we supposed to do now?" she asks.

I finish climbing the stairs and see her point. The door I just passed has led me into an octagonal-shaped waiting room of sorts, with eight separate doors, each featuring a carving of a spider on them.

"I think I remember something about this," PQ says, slightly out of breath from the physical exertion. "In one of the movies or documentaries about this place, they said the town of Dire started out as a mining colony, but once all the gold dried up, Wilson had to find other sources of revenue for the hotel. He incorporated a whorehouse into his hotel and, for some reason, made it spider-themed. I can't remember why."

"Thanks for the history lesson," Shiv says, "but what are we supposed to actually do with that information?"

PQ shrugs. "I don't know. I guess we start looking through the rooms, one by one?"

Shiv sighs impatiently. "That will take ages. Let's just all take a different room and get on with it?"

I don't love the plan of splitting up, but we're all so close to each other, and Shiv's temper seems to be heating up by the minute, so I don't argue. When I volunteer to start on the far right, Shiv takes the far left. PQ opts to stay in the middle, insisting there may be a "spot the difference" type of situation here and he has the best vantage point from the center.

I can't tell if he's being pragmatic or cowardly, but either way, I wish I'd been clever enough to come up with that. The last thing I want is to be surprised by some horrific entity just on the other side of the threshold. I take a deep breath, gingerly turn the knob, and push the door open. The inside of the room looks fairly normal for what I would expect from a turn-of-the-century hotel in the middle of the desert. There's a bed, an armoire, and a bucket prostitutes probably used back in the day for some of the less hygienic parts of their trade.

I check under the bed and in the armoire but find nothing out of the ordinary. Just as I'm ready to start the next room, Shiv reports back similar results, which PQ confirms. Aside from the symbol on the door, the rooms are nearly identical.

It isn't until we each open our second doors that PQ calls out the bed in Shiv's room is different from the rest. Unlike the others, which have four legs reaching the ground, this one has paneling underneath.

"Well, that's interesting," he says. "Maybe we should focus on this room. I bet there's some way to–"

His words get cut off when Shiv starts pressing random wooden panels and turning bedpost knobs. One of them spins, and then we hear the sound of gears. The bed slides on its own accord across the room. Where it once stood is a steep staircase leading down into a dark room below.

"Curiouser and curiouser." PQ squints, trying to make out what could be lurking below. He leans down, placing one foot on the first wooden stair. "*Nope!*" he shouts, literally leaping into the air as he jumps back from the trapdoor.

"What is it?" I ask.

PQ points to the floor, where a brown spider with long legs comes skittering out of the hole. I don't have long to examine it before Shiv stomps a heavy black boot on the creature.

"You gotta be kidding me," Shiv says with a mocking look at PQ. "I've seen you do some of the craziest shit imaginable, and you're telling me that you're afraid of a little spider?"

PQ shakes his head fervently, the color drained from his face. "Not just *any* spiders. That was a brown recluse. Do you know what they can do to you if they bite?"

Shiv shakes her head, conveying more of an attitude of disinterest than lack of knowledge. "So...we'll be careful.

Seriously, PQ, of all things, this is what you're most afraid of? Hang on, is this what you wrote on your questionnaire?"

PQ swallows so hard it nearly sounds like a cartoon gulp. "Remember that time when I took too much acid at the rained-out festival?"

I nod, having heard it many times at this point. "Yeah, and then you spent nine hours hallucinating your death in a van."

With a slight nod, PQ continues. "I never mentioned that I had a tent in the van that ended up being infested with brown recluses. The whole van was full of them. Also, I was seventeen at the time. It ended up being a very formative experience."

Shiv nods impatiently. "So you're saying that you're going to puss out now that you've seen one teensy spider, yeah?"

There's a sigh of frustration, and PQ hops up and down a few times, shaking out his arms and legs. "No, I'll be okay. Can someone else just please take the lead? I need a minute."

"I never pegged you to be such a baby. Shame, really. I kinda liked ya. Fine. I'll lead."

Shiv starts her descent. I follow behind, though as soon as I step down, I notice only my heel rests on the step, and each stair is few and far between. It's closer to a ladder, and each precarious step plunges me further into blackness.

"Blech!" Shiv makes a disgusted noise and flails her arms around below me.

"Are you okay?" I ask.

"Little bastards have really made themselves at home down here. It's full of webs. Hang on, I think I see a light bulb." She reaches out, and I hear the faint jingle of a small metal chain when she gives it a tug. An old, yellowed bulb taps to life.

She wasn't lying. Webs are everywhere, so much so that, as my eyes acclimate to the new light in the room, it almost looks like a static haze. I'm well aware of the danger of brown recluses, but as much as I search for their little bodies scattered amongst the gossamer thicket, or any sense of tiny skittering movement, I find absolutely nothing. Save for the one spider that came out upon our initial reveal of this passage, it appears the room is completely empty of arachnids.

Shiv seems to come to the same conclusion. She gets more aggressive at swatting away the huge, white floating masses during the rest of her descent. As she does this, I keep waiting for a swarm of angry spiders to come surging out of unseen corners, descending upon her en masse for destroying all their hard work.

But nothing happens.

She just continues to clear away webs until her thick black boots are firm on the ground. It's only then I allow myself to take in the actual room. It's small, no larger than the average guest room, except it has two pairs of bunk beds recessed into the walls and several mauve velvet lounge chairs. Along the wall, I see something which immediately makes me call out to our third member.

"Hey, PQ, I think you may want to come down here."

"Pretty sure I'm good where I am," he replies, refusing to even poke his head down the hole.

"You sure? Because I'm about ninety percent sure we just wandered into an opium den." While a couple of the walls feature the built-in bunk beds, one has several mounts for wooden pipes stretching out well over a foot in length. Sitting on a table is an ornate box containing what I assume to be the drug. Behind me, I hear the first of a few hesitant steps down the ladder.

"Holy cow, I've never actually been to an opium den before. This is incredible."

"With all the crazy stuff you've done?" Shiv asks with just a hint of incredulity. "I'd assume you'd crossed opium off your checklist by the time you were a teenager."

PQ shakes his head. "One time, I ordered the special kind of poppy seeds from a guy named Thor in Norway that I met online, and I organized a little get-together to try it. For some reason, I'd always wanted to smoke opium out of a broken light bulb, which ended up being way more trouble than it was worth."

"And how did it go?" Shiv asks.

"The whole thing was a bust. Either Thor sold me bogus poppies, or I didn't prepare them right. Either way, I ended up with a bunch of glass cuts on my hands and never bothered with it again."

"Well, hey, looks like now's your chance."

PQ looks at the webs still taking up a majority of the room and slightly winces. "Under these circumstances, I think I'm good."

I also examine the room a little more closely, and much like every other place we've visited so far, there is more to this space than first meets the eye. A further scan reveals the answer to a question I was secretly begging would never have to be answered. I look up at the ceiling...and discover where all the spiders are.

There is a glass encasement attached to the center. Inside, faint glimmers of tarnished brass occasionally flash between the furious flurry of reddish-brown legs and ovular abdomens. There must be at least a hundred recluses all trapped in the glass box with what I'm becoming increasingly positive is Arthur Wilson's pocket watch.

"Hey, PQ?" I say.

"Yeah?"

"Do me a favor. Don't look up."

"Oh, come on!" he shouts in frustration.

To be fair, I told him not to.

"How the hell are we supposed to get that without killing ourselves?"

"They're just spiders," Shiv says, like it's no big deal.

"Excuse me, but they are not *just* spiders. Do you have any idea what the bite of a brown recluse can do to you? It literally necrotizes the skin. Their venom causes your flesh and muscle to slowly start to eat away at itself over not just hours, but days or even weeks. Sometimes, the only way to stop the spreading is straight up amputation. And let me remind you, that's all from a *single* bite. Do you have any idea what a dozen bites would do to someone?"

I cut in. "I don't mean to be a party pooper, but unless we figure this out quickly, I'm guessing we're all going to be intimately familiar with what those bites feel like."

There have been times since entering this building I wondered if some force is reading my very thoughts. No sooner do I question how this place could possibly get any creepier than the lone light bulb starts to flicker, struggling to keep the room illuminated. It loses the battle, only for a few seconds, but I have a strong and uneasy feeling of what I'm going to see when that light inevitably fights its way back to life.

Even though I'm fully prepared to see Arthur Wilson wielding some terrible implement, he still manages to shock me, though not by appearing right in my face, but by standing very still in a far corner of the room, silently waiting for us to notice him.

I don't know how, but somehow, this is worse than him just coming at us with an axe. It means he is not only evil, but he's patient, clever, and has a plan.

"*Ohmygod.*" PQ's hand flies up to his chest, and he staggers back a few steps when he discovers Arthur with his ghoulish grin in the corner, somewhat obscured behind a gossamer thicket of spider webs.

"You son of a bitch!" Shiv growls, tightening her hands into fists.

*****

Join Shiv on the offensive. Turn to page 94.
Stop Shiv from attacking Arthur. Turn to page 69.

Wilson climbs the stairs, and my heart threatens to beat out of my chest. I'm struggling to come up with a plan to keep Shiv and myself alive, even if it only buys us a few extra minutes.

That's when I realize it.

The box acting as the receptacle for all of Arthur's cursed items is sitting on the lobby bar almost exactly beneath the balcony railing.

I pull the spectacles from my pocket, glancing at Wilson to see how much more time I have left. He's still stalking up the stairs, only now he's reached into his coat and pulled out what appears to be a large rusty hacksaw.

"Is that seriously your plan?" Shiv asks, noticing me holding the spectacles over the railing, pinched between my thumb and first finger.

"How else are we supposed to get down there? Just be ready. As soon as these fall in the box, Wilson will be vulnerable. When that happens, I say we rush him. Maybe we can catch him off guard."

Shiv whines with anxiety, clearly hating my plan but realizing there's little other choice. "Fine. Just don't miss."

I'm about ready to drop the spectacles, but my hand is shaking. At his current rate, we have maybe five seconds until Arthur is upon us. I take one deep inhale, then slowly let my breath out, focusing on calming the tremors in my hand. When the last of my breath exits my lungs, my fingers release and the world goes still, save for a pair of round glasses falling from a balcony.

Come on, come on, come on, my lips chant breathlessly.

The lenses crack when they *clack* against the edge of the box, bouncing back into the air. The glasses do several flips before gravity makes its final determination whether we have a chance or not. After threatening to fall to the lobby floor, the glasses hit the side of the box one more time. A brilliant eruption of purple light explodes from the box.

Now at the top of the stairs, Arthur bares his teeth, like a lion that's just been shot in the shoulder.

"He's weak. Now's the time!" I shout to Shiv, who is standing between me and Wilson.

Without hesitation, Shiv tucks her head and shoulders and charges at Arthur like a football player going for a tackle. She slams into him with so much force, the pair of them go smashing through the wooden banister and plummet down.

"Shiv!" My ankle almost gives out on me. I make the first step to the stairs, and shivers of agony streak up my legs like little lightning bolts. The brown recluse bite is spreading, but there's no time to worry about that now. I grit my teeth and push away the pain in my foot, rushing down the stairs to check on my companion and finish my enemy.

I reach the floor of the lobby, where Shiv groans, her limbs moving around like a jellyfish slowly dying on a beach. The pool of blood spreading on the wood floor around her head scares me more than her moans. "Shiv, can you hear me?"

Her eyes dart around, searching for me despite me standing right over her. Her chest is heaving, fast and shallow. She tries to mumble something, and I'm pretty sure it's "Wilson."

Next to her lies Arthur Wilson, completely motionless, as if he were nothing more than a life-size doll. His eyes are still open, but I no longer feel like they are a pair of all-seeing orbs watching me, no matter where I go. But despite his blank expression, this isn't over until I've pulled that amulet from his neck and smashed it into oblivion.

I start to reach forward, but my hand trembles, and fear surrounds me. The closer I get to the amulet, the more my body hesitates. It's a mistake to be moving this slowly. I know this. But my body won't listen to what my brain is saying.

It's why I only have myself to blame when a hand flies up and grabs my arm. I try to pull away, but Arthur's so strong, it's like his fingers are made of steel. There's a flash of silver, and I'm falling backward, free of his grip.

No, not free of his grip.

Free of my arm.

I look at a circle of bone, muscle, and flesh, all soaked in blood just beneath the elbow. My head collides with the floor, and just like that, the roles between Arthur and I are reversed. He's standing over me with his trademark unhinged smile, pressing a blood-soaked handsaw against my neck.

He saws.

*****

The correct answer was to split up. Turn to page 170.

I read on a bit, then slide the papers away from me, getting a sudden bad feeling about this. "It says that we're going immediately from this to the test shoot, which could take as many as twenty-four hours. It also says I'm not allowed to even let anyone know where I'm about to go. Can I at least call my roommate and tell him I'll be gone for a couple days?"

Lucy shakes her head as if there's nothing she can do. "Unfortunately, that's just the way it is in this business. We're *very* protective of our industry secrets."

Chrissy gives me an annoyed look. "Can you just sign the damn papers already? You're already here."

I shake my head. "Sorry. I thought this was going to take a half a day at most. I have to be on set tomorrow morning."

A hint of a frown touches Lucy's lips. "Well, that's too bad. I think you could have made an excellent test contestant on the show. Here, let me get my assistant, Grimes, to show you out." She knocks on the glass window twice, and a meathead crammed into a suit appears from around the corner.

"Sorry, I'll take an uber home," I tell Chrissy.

The guard leads me to the elevator. Being a tester for a game show sounds fun, but I don't have time for games when there's real work to be done.

We cross the room and step into the elevator. I watch the red numbers over the door while we descend.

3.

2.

1.

B.

B1.

B2.

Hang on. What's with all these basement levels? I got in on the first floor. Shouldn't I be leaving the same way I came? "Aren't we going the wrong way?" I ask.

B3.

B4.

"Back exit," Grimes says.

California doesn't even have basements. How can I be four levels underground? The doors open to a hallway with a flickering orange light. The paint is peeling off the walls, and aside from the hum of electricity, the only sounds down here are our footsteps across a tile floor.

"Hey, guy, where are you taking me?" I ask, this time with a little more force.

The guard grabs me by the shoulder of my gray hoodie, shoves open a white door, and throws me into the room. I'm punched in the nose by the stench of decay. It makes my stomach churn and brings a sour taste to my mouth. I brace myself on a table but find no comfort in seeing what's on it.

There's a camera inside of a rectangular plastic box. The little red light is on, the universal sign for recording. Behind the camera, my face is projected on one of a dozen TVs. The others are filled with elderly looking businessmen, all staring at their screens like they're on one giant Zoom meeting. Some are smiling, while others are leaning in awkwardly.

On my own screen, a figure moves behind me. Grimes steps into frame, reaches into his jacket pocket, then pulls out a pistol. I spin around and stare down the barrel a foot from my face.

Blam!

*****

The correct answer was to sign the NDA. Turn to page 47.

Not only have I heard of Arthur Wilson, I watched both of the '80s *Hell Hotel* movies as part of my cult films course last semester. I even saw the terrible remake, *Murder Mansion*. Lucy looks a little disappointed when I rattle off details about Arthur and his life, about how he built his hotel with a bunch of secret murder rooms so he could torture and experiment on people. I even know all about the Amulet of Duriel, the seemingly mystic artifact Arthur claimed helped him mind control and conjure terrifying creations when he returned to the hotel in the 1960s, with nearly one hundred more victims in tow as his Cult of the Eighth Sin.

It isn't until I'm halfway through describing some of the more brutal torture methods depicted in the movie that it starts to sink in—the place where all the atrocities were committed is the same destination to which we're headed. The things I'm describing now may very well be happening to me soon, or at least some non-fatal facsimile.

The more details I relay–about his prolonged horrific torture across dozens of victims, about his hidden rooms dedicated specifically to keeping harvested diseased body parts as trophies—the more I wish I'd just let Lucy tell her version of the story. Each grim fact I remember from the movies and documentaries is like the link of a chain connecting me to another frightening and morose fact, and I'm suddenly feeling like this is the absolute last place I want to be.

"I'd forgotten about most of that stuff," Chrissy says, remembering halfway through my story that she watched most of these movies with me, though she was probably too stoned at the time to make any lasting memories of it. She gives an awkward half-smile. "I feel like this is going to be messy. I don't love sticky things."

Lucy stiffens her back and rolls her shoulders to show off a professional posture. Her lips curl up into a knowing grin, as if Chrissy has just stumbled onto the setup of an inside joke she wasn't part of.

"Oh, you'll get messy all right. This is splash-zone seating only."

*****

Continue to the hotel. Turn to page 49.

I divert from the path highlighted on our map and find a side door around the corner from where Collins just entered.

"Where the hell are you going?" Chrissy asks, rushing to catch up to me just as I put my hand on the doorknob.

I point at the sign above the door. "They're filming *Unnatural* in there! I just want to take a peek."

"You really shouldn't," she says, pointing to a red light above the door. "It's filming right now. You could get in trouble."

"What was it you said? 'Walk with confidence and everyone will assume you belong'?" I give her a goofy grin, then pull open the door. Working in film and TV is my life's goal. It's why I worked so hard to get into film school in the first place. How can I pass up a chance to see a professional shoot in action?

I step into a room with black walls and a ceiling easily thirty feet tall. The sudden shift from daylight to pure darkness has me nearly blinded, with the exception of an iconic car sitting under a spotlight about twenty feet in front of me—a '67 black convertible Mustang with black and red pony interior. The studio is nearly silent, and in this darkness, I can't see a single other soul in the building.

I figure I might as well get a little closer to the car I see on TV every week. It isn't until I'm stepping into the spotlight that I hear voices to my right.

"Speeding."

"Action. Cue explosives."

My ears prick up at the word "explosives." I look over in the direction of the voices and see a crew of filmmakers sitting wide-eyed behind a plexiglass wall.

We all notice each other a moment too late.

The car bursts into a ball of fire. My skin chars and crackles, and metal shrapnel pierces me in a half-dozen places. An unbelievable force ripples through every cell of my body as I'm blown off my feet and hurled at the wall.

*****

The correct answer was to follow Chrissy. Turn to page 159.

"I mean, they gave us a map for a reason, right?" I say. "Who knows how lost we could get if we just start venturing off in random directions."

"Okay." PQ reorients the map so it correlates with our current heading and relative position to the morgue. "So if we start from here and ignore that path down that way that the map says doesn't exist, we should be following *this* path around a corner to the left, followed by an immediate right."

We walk behind him while he narrates the directions, and at each turn, there seems to be an appropriate landmark. That is, until we follow along a path, searching for a right turn that never seems to come. We backtrack slightly until we come upon a room seemingly directly opposite of where our target room lies.

"Let's get our bearings." I try opening the unlocked door. "If we are where we think we are, there should be a furnace in here."

The room is small, stuffy, and smells strongly of cigar smoke. There is indeed a furnace inside the room, along with a square, brick-lined chute about two feet in diameter running straight up through the ceiling.

"I think this is a chimney." I squint my eyes, trying to make out some details in the dark hole. "There's light up there."

"Okay...," PQ says skeptically. "Don't we want to focus on the task at hand, though? Finding the room with the beaker down here?"

PQ flinches, preparing for another punch when Shiv raises her arm, but instead, she places it on his shoulder.

"No offense, but I'm sick of being in this damned basement. We don't even know if that picture is a real clue."

I nod, agreeing with Shiv. "I'd also feel a lot more comfortable if we could make it into the actual hotel. We can always find the stairs and come back down here if we need to later."

After spending a few moments staring up the hole, PQ asks, "Okay, and how do you propose we get up there?"

"Give me a leg up, and I'll shimmy the rest of the way." Before landing a job in film, I worked on a crew in high school theater. I've crawled, climbed, and scrunched myself into all sorts of tight and dangerous places, and I'm confident I can handle this climb, as long as I can hold proper tension between my feet and the brick wall.

"Here, take this." Shiv pulls a bandana out from her back pocket and hands it to me. "Looks kinda ashy in there. You may want to tie this over your face."

I nod. "Good call. Thanks."

Moments later, PQ and Shiv are boosting me up into the chimney. I'm immediately thankful to have the bandana. My back, legs, and arms press against the walls to give me leverage, stirring up all sorts of soot and dust. It's a game of inches, but I've built up enough stamina over the years from constant grueling hours on set, I can handle it without too much of a sweat. I see the faded maroon ceiling and bookshelves of a room just above me. I'm able to get my hands on the ledge of what feels like a fireplace and pull myself up.

There, I find myself face-to-face with a man in a brown bowler hat and round glasses revealing empty white eyes. I can not only see, but *feel* his malevolent smile beneath a bushy mustache. His right hand produces a scalpel glinting in the light of what appears to be a small study or library. I glance back down, wondering if I should let myself fall rather than endure whatever the spirit of Arthur Wilson has planned for me. It's a solid twenty-foot drop, and my legs are already shaking from exhaustion.

A slow agony slides across my finger when Wilson draws a line down my pointer with his blade. Blood runs in equal parts along both sides of the digit, and I gasp in pain. I try to prop myself back up with my legs, but I no longer have traction. My boots are slipping against the sooty wall, kicking up clouds of dust that burn my eyes and make me cough.

Wilson brings the knife down on my middle finger, starting at the back knuckle and drawing it all the way to the nail. I scream, and my hand gives out. Suddenly, I'm a ragdoll tumbling every which way against the walls of the chimney, flying headfirst for the furnace room.

*****

The correct answer was to ignore the map. Turn to page 60.

When nobody else volunteers, I decide to *not* be the one dissenting voice in the crowd. Instead, I follow Lucy and the others into an old doctor's office. There are multiple wires running from the back of the building to some clamp lights, keeping the office from feeling too dark. Another wire runs to a small camera lens not so subtly attached to the wall by a binder clip. Most of the windows have so much dust on them, they barely let in any more than a warm ambient glow.

"Please excuse the mess. We're still in the process of setting up our crew spaces and refurbishing the town. During your playtest, you may find some cameras' lighting equipment or crew gear that hasn't been fully installed. Basically, don't touch anything that looks expensive. Clear?"

Everyone nods.

"Great. Then let's get started, shall we?"

Lucy gestures to a series of papers laid out on a metal surgical table so rusted, it looks just as brown as the crumbling wood surrounding it. Three maps sit in the center. They're labeled "Basement," "First Floor," and "Second Floor," the paper yellow and faded, with fold lines delicate enough to tear, if one were to lift them too quickly. The blueprints themselves are only semi-helpful; half the rooms have been erased entirely, and there are pencil sketches carving out new rooms or overlapping existing ones in bizarre ways. Even with a partial guide, the place looks like a labyrinth I could easily get lost in, and that's *before* factoring in all the hidden torture and death rooms which surely aren't depicted in these maps.

"The rules of the game are simple," Lucy says. "The ghost of Arthur Wilson, America's most prolific serial killer, is roaming the halls of The Propitius Hotel. Up until now, his spirit has been relatively harmless, until a group of urban explorers made their way into the hotel recently and discovered the source of Wilson's power—the Amulet of

Duriel. After nearly sixty years of dormancy, these explorers managed to reawaken something dark and hungry inside the hotel. The urban explorers never made it out of the building, and their bodies were never recovered."

Before continuing, Lucy lets her last words linger a few seconds for dramatic flair.

"To make matters worse, mediums across the country have been reporting a growing malignant force at The Propitius. Whatever energy those recent victims gave to Wilson has caused him to grow exponentially in power. With the amulet at his disposal, there's no telling what damage he could do to the living world, if he grows strong enough. That's where the four of you come in. Your job is to stop the spirit of Arthur Wilson before it's too late, by destroying the Amulet of Duriel that he possesses. Of course, there's one catch."

"There always is," PQ says with eager anticipation.

"You see, Wilson keeps the amulet safely around his neck; however, his spirit is incorporeal. You can't touch him."

"Then what's the big deal? If he can't touch us, then where's the danger?" I ask.

"Oh, no." Lucy raises a condescending finger in the air. "Just because you can't touch him doesn't mean *he* can't touch *you*."

Shiv nods. "So, it's like stripper rules then, yeah?"

"Not quite," Lucy says with a sly grin. "Most strippers can't slit your throat with a scalpel, or strap you into a drill desk."

"What's a drill desk?" PQ asks, raising his hand.

Lucy's smile grows even more mischievous. "Let's hope you don't find out. The only way you'll be able to dispel the magic keeping Wilson's ghost invulnerable is by collecting a series of his personal items that he had in life. You must search the hotel to find his spectacles, pocket watch, and journal. Then, place them all in the special Ectoplasmic Containment Unit found somewhere inside the house. In order to recover these sacred items, you'll have to solve puzzles, complete challenges, and most importantly, survive long enough to make him vulnerable, defeat him, then steal and shatter the Amulet of Duriel. Make sense?"

PQ shrugs. "Sounds like a pretty standard, non-denominational exorcism to me. Let's do it."

Lucy claps her hands together. "Perfect. Then, unless you have any questions, this is where I leave you."

"Hang on," I say, waving my hand and dreading the question I'm about to ask. "Aren't you going to let us into the hotel first?"

It's clearly a performative laugh, but Lucy manages to pull it off well. "Why, all doors in and out of The Propitius are locked. You'll have to find your own way in." Lucy strides across the room, her red high heels clacking against the rotten, warped wood panels on the floor. She opens the front door and turns back, just before shutting us in. "I'll give you one hint to get started. This clinic belonged to Arthur's father. Word is, they built a hidden passage to transport bodies from here down to the morgue in the hotel basement. Good luck." With that, Lucy gives us all a wink, then shuts the door behind her, followed by the sound of a deadbolt lock turning for good measure.

PQ carefully folds the maps along their well-worn crease lines and tucks them into the back pocket of his shorts. "All right, everybody know what we're doing?"

Chrissy looks over to PQ as if she just got caught playing with her phone in class. "Sorry, did anyone else completely miss that?"

"Miss what?" I ask.

"Like, the whole thing. I'm sorry, but as soon as I hear someone start talking about backstory and rules, I just kind of tune out naturally. What are we doing again?"

I bury my hands in my face with a dramatic gesture, half in actual frustration and half to embarrass my friend. "This is like the time I brought you to board game night all over again."

Chrissy shakes her head, like she's got some cobwebs stuck in her brain and she's trying to rustle them out. "It's fine. I'm more of a visual learner anyways. I'll just pick it up as we go along."

This is *exactly* why she wanted me to join her in this game to begin with. While she made an excellent extra on sets, where her direction was "stand here, look busy," this production is on an entirely different level. Chrissy's not likely to be much help, but it's nice we have someone as capable as PQ.

In fact, he's already searching the room, inspecting the floors carefully. "If there's a passage leading to the main house, it's gotta be through some kind of hatch or loose floorboards," he says. It doesn't take long to find two squares cut into the floor, one on either side of the operating table.

"And check this out." I examine a rusty lever sitting right next to the table and do my best to give it a pull, but it won't budge.

"Come on, Jer. Put your back into it," Shiv says, clearly unimpressed by my feat of strength.

"I don't think it's because of rust." I give it a few jiggles and feel some wiggle room, until the lever reaches a clear stopping point. "I think there's something keeping it locked."

Chrissy yawns. "Do you think this whole thing is going to be like this?" She rubs her eyes and sighs in a way I know all too well. It's the move she makes when she's over whatever task she's doing and has decided she wants to go back to her campus apartment and get stoned. She rests both her elbows on the operating table, then cradles her head in her hands.

Her elbows sink a few inches, and there's the sound of a satisfying click.

"Whoa, I think that's it," I say. "The crank won't work unless there's a body putting pressure on the table.

Shiv nods, looking slightly impressed. "All right, smart guy. You wanna be the one to test that theory?

*****

Volunteer to go first. Turn to page 59.
Chicken out. Turn to page 6.

I look to Chrissy, who is already halfway through with her questionnaire. "Hey, is this kind of stuff normal?"

She nods. "Yeah, you usually have to sign a million deals agreeing to secrecy before you can do anything fun. I can't even tell you about half the celebrities I've met." Chrissy casts a quick look up to me and wiggles her eyebrows playfully.

I sign the NDA, then move on to the questionnaire. It starts simple, asking about my education, strengths, weaknesses, etc. I answer as honestly as I can, until I get to one asking: "What is your biggest fear?"

For a moment, I'm nine years old, sitting on my bed, my brother, Brian, crying for help on the other side of a collapsed, burning ceiling beam. I want to get to him, want to help him out of the house, but I'm so small and it's so hot. There's nothing I can do. Even the thought of fire brings up memories of his screams, images of his burnt face, while I sat helplessly and eventually escaped out the bedroom window.

Nope, can't write that. I just put down I'm afraid of snakes, even though they don't particularly bother me. It seems like a believable-enough answer.

Within five minutes of finishing our paperwork, we are led back into the elevator by Lucy and the big man in the suit, then outside to a black van.

"The location we're shooting at is a few hours' drive from here—an old, abandoned mining town called Dire. The show is going to be called *Slashtag*. Well, either that or *The Grind House*. You're about to do a test run of what is going to be the most immersive reality competition of all time. You, along with two other contestants, will work together in one of the most haunted buildings in America. Your goals will be to solve riddles, complete challenges, and follow clues to exorcise a particularly nasty ghost that's been haunting the place since the 1960s. If you can complete all the challenges and dispel the spirit within twenty-four hours, you'll win the grand prize—or at least you would, if this were the actual show. But if you get caught by the ghost, or one of the many other supernatural dangers in the house, you'll be added to the list of his victims and eliminated from the competition.

"We're thinking of getting celebrities to be contestants on the actual series, but for now, the goal is to make sure all the pieces are coming together properly. You'll be participating in an abridged version of the competition, to test out certain features we're trying to implement. I hope you like horror movies because you're about to take part in the scariest reality competition of all time."

Chrissy and I are both casual horror fans, enough that we see the major tentpole flicks and most of the indie stuff A24 puts out. While it's not exactly my genre of choice, I've worked on several student films and studied enough film history to think I'll be able to separate my natural fear response from the knowledge everything happening in there is the product of movie magic.

"So, who's the ghost? What's the story behind this haunted house?"

That same mischievous grin spreads across Lucy's lips. "Have you ever heard of Arthur Wilson and The Propitius Hotel?"

*****

Ask for the full story. Turn to page 66.

Explain that you're an expert on Arthur and his history (I've read *Slashtag*). Turn to page 35.

After several hours of driving through the desert, we pull off the highway onto an unmarked dirt path, and it's only then I notice there's a second black Suburban following us. It eats our dust as we carve a path through a loosely defined road in the sand, heading literally toward the middle of nowhere.

"Well, this isn't at all ominous," Chrissy says. Aside from our two black vehicles, there's nothing but desert stretching for miles all around us.

"If you think this is desolate, you should see Kinsin, Arizona. I crewed a student film there once, and the only motel didn't even have indoor plumbing." I try to remind myself I've worked under long and difficult conditions before, equally hoping to convince myself rough conditions don't bother me, even though there's a growing sense of unease inside my chest.

It's almost as if time slows on the dirt road. Without any landmarks or traces of civilization, it becomes almost impossible to keep track of time. Lucy confiscated our phones and wallets before leaving the office as part of a security protocol, and it's difficult to see the car's clock from the back seat. After what seems like several more hours, we pull up to a weather-worn wooden board with the name of the town: Dire, California.

The name feels appropriate. The town consists of little more than a strip of shabby buildings from the Old West. I'm able to make out faded signs for a mining supply store, a bank, and a sheriff's station. I'm so distracted trying to make out the words, I don't notice the looming mansion in front of us until Chrissy taps my shoulder.

The two-story Propitius Hotel dwarfs the town. It's so large, I can't see more than the first floor, so I lean forward and squint through the front windshield. The building stands at complete odds with the rest, almost as though it has been removed from time and space altogether. While Dire is pretty much what I'd expect from a mining town abandoned nearly one hundred years ago, The Propitius is a pristine, Gothic, Tudor-style hotel that almost looks like it belongs at Disneyland. I roll down my window so I can stick my head outside and look at the building in all its glory. It might as well be a castle. Massive octagonal towers covered in stained glass windows climb up the building's four corners, each ending in a sharp, steepled roof.

Despite the seemingly endless amount of intricate glasswork and Gothic architecture to admire, my eyes gravitate toward the bright red door, the last barrier nearly 140 people crossed before meeting their end. The fact the door is red almost makes it seem vampiric, drawing me in, only to reveal something monstrous inside.

The SUV pulls to a stop, and even though I step out into a cloudless desert in the middle of summer, a chill runs through me. One step closer to entering the building.

"Would you look at that? It's just like in the film!" a voice says from behind me.

I turn. A pair around my age climbs out of the Suburban following us. The woman talking speaks with an Irish accent. Her hair is punked up into a series of liberty spikes. She's wearing all black, except for a cutoff denim vest absolutely covered in rock band patches ranging from the classic Misfits skull to the Roman numerals IX, for the recent metal sensation, Ice Nine Kills. She's tall, even without her platform boots or spiked hair, and has broad shoulders, like she's a swimmer or a boxer.

I welcome the distraction, casting my eyes away from the hotel and meeting this woman. "Hi, I'm Jeremy," I say, putting out my hand.

"Shiv." She takes mine in a firm grasp and gives it a single shake.

"Chrissy," my friend says, stepping in next to me.

Shiv nods across the vehicle, where someone just shut the driver's-side door. "That's PQ over there."

"PQ Mezrow?" Chrissy asks with a growing smile of recognition.

From the side of the car steps a slightly overweight guy with a goatee and cowboy hat, an alligator skull adorning it. I smile too, welcoming the surprisingly friendly face, while not at all being shocked to find him at a place like this. PQ graduated from our film school last year, and it's no exaggeration to say that, in his time at our college, he became a literal legend. If there was an insane story involving fire-juggling clown strippers, an impromptu Shrek-themed rave, or a screening of *IT* in an actual sewer under L.A., PQ was at the center of it.

Chrissy knows him much better than me, having spent a significant amount of her time in college partying while I was on weekend film sets, but he greets me with as much gusto as he does her, offering us both deep and sincere hugs.

"Shiv and I met at a party in an old insane asylum, where I had managed to find actual recordings of Bulgarian prisoners screaming in agony after decades of solitary confinement."

"It was pretty wicked," Shiv agrees, giving PQ's fist a pound.

"Oh, excellent. You all know each other already," Lucy says, in a hard-to-read tone. "This game is all about teamwork, so it'll be nice having a group that already has some rapport." To my surprise, instead of ushering us toward The Propitius, she raises a hand to a barely standing doctor's clinic at the edge of town. "Now, if everyone's ready to learn the rules to the game, please follow me to the clinic. If any of you need to use the restroom first, we've got the plumbing running in the bank."

*****

Head to the clinic. Turn to page 42.
Find the bathroom in the bank. Turn to page 14.

*****

While I am far from being the master of knowing horror tropes, the one thing I do remember is you always stick together, no matter what. "Hang on. We're coming with you."

The three of us cross the threshold into the guest room. PQ beelines it through the open door to the bathroom, and he lets out a cheer of success when the faucet turns on and clear water comes running from the spout. I'm keeping an eye on him, and the room, just to make sure there's no looming threat about to pop out.

It's much smaller than even the crummiest motel room I've stayed in for out-of-town film shoots. There's a twin-sized bed, a tall wooden armoire for clothes, and not much else.

"Ey, Jeremy, careful not to venture too far in." Shiv stands at the far end of the room, staring at something just beyond the large Armoire. "You might have quite a fright if you come any closer."

There's an edge to her voice telling me she's screwing with me. On one hand, I'm too on edge making sure PQ is safe to fall for her diversion. However, curiosity gets the better of me, and I take several steps forward to see what nasty prank she's pulling. I let out an audible groan when I realize she's pointing to a standing mirror in the corner.

"Just wanted to give you a heads-up, in case you have another terrifying encounter with yourself." Her thin lips carve a sharp smile across her face.

"Very funny," I say, looking into the dirty mirror at Shiv and my reflection.

The lights go out, leaving us in complete darkness.

"Hey, what gives?" PQ shouts from the bathroom. "I'm not done scrubbing black lung out of my fingernails here."

"We're not doing this—" I start to reply but am interrupted when the lights struggle, flickering back to life.

By the time they come back on, I'm looking at a very different image in the mirror. Shiv is still standing right beside me, except there's no *me* reflected in the glass. Instead, a pair of white, hollow eyes framed in round spectacles stare back. It's the ghost of Arthur Wilson, in full brown tweed suit and bowler hat. If this wasn't enough of a shock, his grin is a nightmare of mangled brown teeth jutting in all directions.

"Oh my God," I say, urging my feet to carry me far from this lunatic's reflection, but my legs won't move. In fact, the more I try to force myself to do anything, I find myself completely paralyzed. The one thing I can feel moving—and it scares me most of all—is a maddening grin tugging at the corners of my lips, as if someone has shoved fingers into my mouth, spreading them to the point where my lips crack from the painful stretching.

"All right, joke's over, weirdo," Shiv says, clearly not seeing what I am.

I try to warn her about the mass murderer who is controlling me from beyond the looking glass, but with my mouth held open as it is, I can't make much more than the nonsense grunts I would give at a dentist's office.

"Seriously, Jeremy, that's enough," she says, with just a whisper of concern creeping into her voice.

The water shuts off in the bathroom, and in the mirror, I watch PQ wander into the bedroom, toweling his hands. "Did I just walk in on something?" he asks awkwardly.

"I don't know. I was just ribbing him for being scared of his own reflection, and then he sort of froze there with a creepy smile."

"Jeremy, buddy, you feeling okay?" PQ asks, hazarding a step toward me.

Wilson winks at me, and against my own volition, my eye squeezes shut, matching his.

PQ takes another step and tries to jostle me out of it by placing a hand on my shoulder from behind.

I let out another grunt of pain when Wilson forces my smile to the point blood runs from the corners of my lips. My hand follows his into my jacket pocket and grabs the handle of something cold and metal.

My hand jerks up and behind my shoulder. The mirror guides the tip of the scalpel directly into PQ's eye, the blade piercing his soft, squishy organ as if it were a grape.

He screams, reels back. Before Shiv has a chance to respond, my arm swings in a wide arc, slitting her throat. She falls to her knees, holding her hands to her neck. What seems like gallons of blood pump between the feeble dams of her fingers.

The scalpel falls to the floor, but Wilson's not done with me. My hands grab the mirror, and Wilson forces me to slam my head into the glass. Once, twice, three times, until I look back at a hundred tiny vignettes of a face between the cracks. It's no longer Arthur Wilson, but rather someone else. There's a huge shard of glass sticking out of his forehead, and blood has covered at least half of his face.

It's strange—one of my last thoughts before I fall to the ground is, I don't even recognize my own reflection in the mirror anymore.

*****

The correct answer was to give PQ some privacy to clean up.
Turn to page 117.

I think about the question from all sides and re-read the book entry. "Given what I know about Wilson from the movies, he seemed like he was mostly using medical experimentation as an excuse to do really horrific stuff to innocent people. I think the black lung stuff is a red herring and he'd be more focused on horrifically murdering innocent people. Let's go for Daniel's liver and kidneys."

We grab the jars for his other organs. They're all easy to find—part of a set of about ten jars filled with pieces of Daniel, all clustered together.

"You ready to pop another top?" Shiv asks PQ.

"Already on it."

He tries, and fails, to twist the cap off Daniel's Liver. PQ's hands are still wet from the last jar, and it's clearly making things difficult for him. He grips the lid through his shirt to get a good enough traction. When it finally pops open, rotten chemicals splash all over his stomach and arms.

"Ow!" PQ hisses, placing the opened jar on the table and frantically rubbing the preservative liquid off himself. "This stuff kind of burns."

"Did the other one feel that way?" I ask.

"No, it felt like thick water. This stuff almost feels like it's some kind of an acid." PQ rubs his hands and arms against his shirt, trying to towel them off.

"Do you think maybe that's a sign that we're on the wrong path? The first one didn't seem to burn like this."

"Only one way to find out." Shiv reaches into the jar, grabs the big purple hunk of meat, and places it in the bowl. "Jesus effin' Christ, that stings!" Shiv shouts, now wiping her hand aggressively against her denim vest. Now that the liver is no longer obscured by the murky chemicals, I notice what appear to be seam lines on the side, as if it were made from a plastic mold. It looks rubbery, fake. We've been fooled by a phony organ.

PQ groans, and that's when I notice the growing dark stain around his gut. It's more than twice the size of the splash from opening the jar. It's also leaking. He seems to notice it too, and when he lifts his shirt, part of his stomach has been eaten away. A yellow foam bubbles around a red mass in the middle of his gut, and blood is oozing out from all sides, making it hard to see what's fully going on.

"Hey, guys, I don't think we picked the right—Hurghhhh." PQ doubles over in agony, and red sticky ropes come tumbling out of his stomach. They hit the floor with a wet splat.

It becomes even more clear this was a mistake when Shiv lets out a grunt of pain through gritted teeth. She flaps her hand around, as if trying to air-dry it, and sends something flying, which hits me in the cheek.

I pick the small red chip off the ground, then quickly drop it. It's an entire fingernail. I look back at her hand—she's lost more than just her nails. The skin itself seems to be wicking off her fingers, like wax on a burning candle. Globs of liquefied skin, blood, and tissue ooze down her bright red hand. She screams, her eyes wide, and she stares at the melting carnage.

The lights flicker out, and we're all in the dark. When they come back on, we're no longer alone in the room.

There's a man standing opposite us, in a surgeon's garb. He's wearing his iconic round spectacles and has a large bushy mustache. There's no mistaking it—we are standing in the presence of the spirit of Arthur Wilson, one of America's most sadistic serial killers.

PQ and Shiv seem to be in too much agony to notice his arrival, but I can't resist staring into his blank white eyes. He curls his lips into a smile, which I can only make out at the corners of either end of his mustache. Arthur reaches above his head and pulls down a hose I hadn't noticed coming from the ceiling. Before I even have a chance to warn the others, he turns a crank on the nozzle, and a green fluid comes spraying out, looking identical to the contents of the jars.

Yup, it's definitely acid, I tell myself while I'm getting doused in the stuff. Within seconds, every inch of me sizzles from the chemicals. An unbearable blistering pain lights up every one of my synapses, and the one consolation is, it doesn't take long before the world fades to black.

*****

Try again. Turn to page 65.

"I guess I'm as good a guinea pig as any." I climb onto the table and lie down, like one of Wilson's patients from over one hundred years ago. It isn't until I'm already on the table that my heart begins to pound, and it truly sinks in this is where it all really starts. There's no going back now.

"One...two..." Shiv starts to count me off but pulls the lever before she gets to three.

My lungs leap into my throat when the table tips in the opposite direction I'm expecting. I go flying headfirst through an open trapdoor and onto a metal slide.

Plunging into absolute pitch-black, I twist and turn down this ancient corpse chute. My back thrums with pain, passing over what must be bolts of some kind holding the thing together. It may just be an illusion because of the air pushing against my speedy descent, but a distinct chill runs through me. I try my best not to think about the dozens, or possibly hundreds, of bodies that have taken this ride before me.

The top of my head smacks into the side on a sharp turn. I need to slow down or catch myself before I crash headfirst into wherever this slide leads, so I press my hands against the ceiling. It's made of carved rock, shredding my flesh and ripping my palms into ribbons.

Suddenly I'm weightless, hurling through the air with nothing but momentum on my side, blue lights above me. My head slams into the floor at an awkward angle, twisting it to the side with a loud crack.

*****

The correct answer was to chicken out. Turn to page 6.

"I don't care what that stupid piece of paper says," Shiv argues. "I'm looking at a path here that takes us straight to that room."

A silence hangs over us, and they look to me with expectations of a decision being made. I lean into my gut. My experience running countless all-night film sets with herds of exhausted, overworked students has taught me how to take quick decisive action.

"I agree with Shiv. Let's take the shortcut. If we're all doomed anyways, it won't make that big a difference in the grand scheme, and if there *is* a way out of this, I'd rather figure it out sooner than later."

The three of us leave the morgue and take our first left into uncharted territory. After a quick right, we find ourselves in front of a door with a tarnished brass placard reading: "Storage."

"Unless this is where Arthur Wilson kept his science equipment, I'd hardly say the picture of the beaker on the map represents a storage room," PQ says. "I'm not even seeing a storage room on the legend. Maybe we took a wrong turn somewhere and should go back."

Hesitation is not a good look on PQ, and I try to cajole him into being the gung-ho weirdo I've always known him to be. "Where's your adventurous spirit, PQ? I've seen you take Nepalese mad bee honey, then go to a screening of *Eraserhead*. Are you telling me you're afraid of a storage closet?"

PQ raises his hands defensively. "Are you kidding? You would *have* to be a crazy person to not be shitting yourself right now! I'll be the first to admit I'm absolutely terrified, and that's coming from someone who once licked way too much acid off a strange woman's finger at a rained-out festival, then spent nine hours watching my own death play out on repeat inside of an Astro van."

"So, what do you want us to do?" Shiv asks. "Stand around here with our thumbs up our asses?"

PQ shrugs. "If you're so brave, why don't one of you two go in?"

Now it's my turn to play defense. "I was just trying to get everyone on the same page. I don't want to force you to do something if you're not comfortable. I just thought you'd know what to do in this kind of situation."

"Well, I can honestly say this is the first time where crispy, burny death or legendary Irish folklore ghosts are things to be concerned about."

"You two are both pussies, you know that?" Shiv says, shoving her shoulder into me to make way as she pushes through the door.

I follow her into a room that smells like an old folks' home. The dim orange hum of the hallway turns into a clinical blue. I inspect what houses a very different kind of collection than I was expecting. There are dozens of jars placed along a series of wooden shelves lining the storage closet. Each glass jar contains an internal organ bathed in a liquid ranging in color from pale yellow to a murky green. There's a heart, a brain, a number of curled-up baby fetuses of various sizes, and a number of parts which I couldn't even hazard to guess. Considering what I've seen so far, I have no doubt in my mind these are all real and not TV replicas. Nothing about this sick contest feels even remotely fake.

As I'm making my way through shelf after shelf of pickled human remains, I notice something which makes me believe we're absolutely in the right place. A book sits on a table, opened to a page written by hand. It's something between a diary and a medical textbook, with several diagrams of human anatomy sketched out in ink taking up the majority of the right page. It must be Arthur Wilson's journal—one of the three artifacts needed for our mission to stop his ghost and end this nightmare for us all.

Of course, there's a catch. The book, much like all the preserved organs around me, is encased in glass. There's a lock at the base, with three bolts securing it in place. To the case's immediate right sits three metal bowls, each cemented to the table.

"Hey, guys, look at this," I say, drawing their attention to the book. As soon as they've all crowded around me, there's a loud slam behind us. The door to the storage room has shut itself of its own accord.

"Cool. That's definitely not super ominous or anything," PQ says.

"It just means we're on the right track. I bet whatever's written here is a clue for how to retrieve the journal. If we read the page, it'll tell us what we need to put into those bowls."

"I'm sorry. Are you suggesting we actually reach into some of these jars and put things in those bowls?"

"Afraid of getting your hands a little dirty? I thought you were into all that gross kind of stuff," Shiv says.

"Oh no, don't get me wrong," PQ replies. "I'm definitely going to be touching one of the disembodied penises on this shelf over here. I agree there are some once-in-a-lifetime opportunities you just *have* to take. I'm mostly concerned about what's going to happen if we place the wrong parts in the wrong bowls. No offense, Jeremy, but I'm having some flashbacks of Chrissy choosing the wrong door in the morgue, and it didn't turn out particularly awesome for her."

I grit my teeth and try to push that trauma out of my head before it has a chance to grow roots. "It seems like there's only one way to find out. Let's see what we can make of this." I return my attention to the book and start reading the passage on the left page aloud.

"September twenty-eight, 1913. Aside from accidents from collapses and explosions within the mines, the most common condition that patients suffer from is the black lung. While Father toils away at thinking of preventative measures for the ailment, I am doing the real work in trying to find a cure. I found a youngster not too long ago who had stopped by The Propitius Hotel for lodging on his way north, who claimed he had never inhaled so much as a cigarette in his life. Said he was a church man by the name of Daniel Lawrence. Of course, I needed him for my collection as a control sample. Not only did he provide me with a healthy set of lungs, his abstinence from alcohol provided me with a pristine set of kidneys and a liver.

"I'm fortunate to have come upon such a sample, as now I have a fairly comprehensive understanding of the different stages of the disease. Bill Humber provided me lungs with a moderate case, while old Jebediah Hess is preserved as an example of lungs in a terminal state. Perhaps if there were some way to purify the particles in the lungs without having to remove them first, I could help save some of the poor souls already suffering from the disease. In the meantime, I will continue to test lung-cleaning techniques on live subjects, via surgically opening the chest cavity and observing the lungs' reactions to my trials in real time."

"Jesus, I'd hate to see what lung-cleaning techniques look like," Shiv says. "So, what do you think he's getting at here, besides being a sick bastard? He spends a lot of time waxing poetic about this Daniel fella. Do you think he wants us to put all the healthy parts in the bowls to celebrate his trophies?"

"I don't know," PQ says. "While he was pretty excited about the clergyman, the primary topic of the entry, in my opinion, was the black lung, which I would think means we're supposed to show the progression of the disease."

I'm not ready to come to a decision yet, though I can feel the tension in the room starting to point in my direction. "Either way, it seems like we need to start with Daniel's lungs, right? So let's start there while we think about the puzzle."

We search the room and see each jar has a lid with faded handwriting on it featuring a subject's name and a date. We're after lungs, so I skip by all the disembodied hands, heads, babies, and genitals and head straight for the wall loaded up with internal organs. I know I'm looking for one of the healthier-looking ones, but considering my non-existent medical knowledge, mixed with the fact these all look like they've somewhat decayed over the last hundred years, it's very hard to tell one organ's health from another.

"Got the lungs!" Shiv says, grabbing a jar from the shelf. "Looks like the rest of Pastor Daniel's here too, in case we want to go that route."

"Let's start with the lungs and see what happens," I suggest.

Shiv places the jar on the table, next to the bowls. "All right, weirdo," she says to PQ, "time to get your hands dirty."

To PQ's credit, as much as he spoke earlier about being afraid, he wastes no time opening the ancient jar of lungs, as if they were pickles he'd just brought home from the store. It's a good thing these parts are labeled. I was hunting for something that looked like a pair of lungs from the pictures I've seen in textbooks and stuff, but in reality, it's just a bisected slice of orange-brown tissue with a bunch of little white roots spreading throughout.

The smell when PQ opens the jar is overwhelming. It's like I'm inhaling a super-potent mixture of kimchi, vinegar, and formaldehyde. To his credit, PQ reaches in without hesitation, carefully cupping the section of lungs in his hand, then gingerly places it into the bowl.

At the base of the glass container, a single deadbolt releases.

"Looks like we're on the right track." PQ wipes his slimy hand off on his cargo shorts.

"All right, Jeremy, decision time, and you're the tiebreaker," Shiv says. "Do we keep adding pieces of Daniel to the bowls, or do we go on the hunt for diseased lungs?"

*****

Place Daniel's healthy parts in the bowls.
Turn to page 56.
Place the different sets of lungs in the bowls.
Turn to page 161.
Forget the puzzle. Smash the glass case with one of the jars.
Turn to page 156.

"He was a serial killer, right?" I vaguely remember a movie from ten or so years ago based on a true story. It was called *Murder Mansion* and got something like a thirteen percent on *Rotten Tomatoes*. It starred that douchey actor Landon Keating too, so I never really bothered to learn more.

Lucy clears her throat and sits up straight in her chair, adopting a TV-host persona.

"In the late 1800s, an East Coast surgeon named John Wilson established Dire as a gold mining town, turning his modest wealth into a small fortune. His son, Arthur, wanted to be a surgeon, just like him. It started out well enough; however, Arthur proved to have an obsession with making scientific advances in medicine, using sick or injured patients as guinea pigs. His father forbade him to practice medicine. However, Arthur was both brilliant and determined. He instead focused his efforts on building a hotel that would turn Dire from a tiny gold operation into a destination. He named the building The Propitius, hoping to bring in good fortune.

"And good fortune it did. Not only did The Propitius operate as a hotel, this massive building became the center point of town. It had a saloon, gambling hall, restaurant, barber, bookshop, even a whorehouse. But all of that was just a cover. You see, when Arthur had the hotel built, he installed hidden spaces throughout the buildings—rooms for torture, dissection, and hideous scientific experiments. He'd lure unsuspecting miners to his hotel, loners who'd set out to strike it rich, and then kidnap them from their rooms at night. It was suspected he killed nearly forty victims between 1906 and 1928. He only stopped his practice when an explosion in his underground distillery revealed over a dozen buried corpses."

She doesn't just tell a story; she delivers a monologue ready for prime time. Bits of this story are coming back. I remember parts of it from the trailer to *Murder Mansion* and pieces from documentaries that were popular about the subject years ago. I nod my head to show I'm catching on. "Right, and then he got away and came back, like, twenty years later, as a Jim Jones type."

"Something like that." Lucy looks only slightly perturbed about me interrupting the speech she was surely rehearsing for the show's eventual premiere. "It's unknown when, but rumor says that Arthur found an artifact known as the Amulet of Duriel that gave him supernatural abilities. He could control minds or even conjure a person's greatest fear, right in front of them. In the '60s, he returned to the hotel as Reverend Arthur Sutter, along with one hundred followers of a cult he had formed known as the Church of the Eighth Sin. It's rumored that, with his amulet, he performed all sorts of horrific acts on his followers for nearly a year before gassing them all to death and taking his own life."

My mouth is dry. I try to swallow, but it does nothing to alleviate the situation. "So that's the ghost we have to try to take on? Arthur Wilson? In his actual hotel?"

Lucy nods. "It's been refurbished, and we're in the process of installing cameras and microphones throughout. But yes, we're headed toward the real house."

"I don't know how I feel about this," I say.

"What do you mean?"

"It's one thing to indulge in scary stories that are fiction, but I've always found it to be in poor taste to fetishize actual mass murderers. For one thing, they have real victims, actual people who have been affected by this. Reveling in the deaths of innocent people feels pretty distasteful to me."

"Well, it's a good thing you're not going to be on the actual show, then." Lucy snaps out of her host voice, sounding impatient with me.

Chrissy jostles my shoulder. "Whether it's us or some other shmoe, this show's going to happen either way. It might as well be you that gets some money out of it. Besides, we signed those NDAs. No one's going to know you had anything to do with this anyways."

I nod, feeling uneasy, like a crack is forming in the partition between fantasy and reality.

*****

Continue to the hotel. Turn to page 49.

"Wait!" I throw my arm across Shiv's chest, like a mom instinctually protecting her child when slamming on car brakes. I fully expect her to fight me on this, but in the moment between her rash decision and my attempted denial, it seems she noticed the same thing I did.

Even Arthur's presence itself is a trap. A door has opened beneath his feet, and he is hovering in mid-air, goading us to try something, but we aren't falling for it.

Arthur winks at us, as if to say, "Hey, can't blame a guy for trying." Even though his eyes are a pair of empty white voids, it feels as if he is staring directly into me, and the smile creeping along his face makes my stomach go sour. I wonder what he's seeing in me that brings him such glee.

Without diverting his glance, he reaches an open hand of long, bony fingers and wraps them around the handle of a large gramophone standing next to him. His head slowly nods, and a muffled voice speaks, constantly punctuated by the crackles and pops of the antique spinning record. I can only assume it's his own voice, not just providing us with an audio account of his experiments, but likely a clue as to how to retrieve the pocket watch.

"October 17, 1922. With the gold mine long since dried up and prohibition in full effect across the nation, The Propitius stands, now more than ever, as a place of solace for those seeking fortune and debauchery. With the rest of Dire mostly abandoned, my hotel stands as a singular draw for the clientele I seek to attract. Gone are the days of mingling with guests to discover their ties, or lack thereof. Gone are the days of waiting patiently for an opportunity to find the right subjects. In fact, in the absence of Mother and Father, I have even formed a partnership with a madam, Geraldine Webb, to convert their old chambers into a whorehouse, to further attract passersby who won't be missed.

"I've grown particularly fond of the opium den she suggested building. It's made collecting victims so effortless, I almost feel ashamed for taking them from their drug-induced catatonia. However, there is science to be done and a hunger that must be satisfied, so I must seize on any and all opportunities.

"Recently, one such opportunity has arisen, as a series of highly venomous spider bites have been reported around the hotel. Since I am also the attending physician, I've seen the devastating long-term suffering the venom from the arachnids can cause. Perhaps I can find a way to harness its caustic power for medical purposes. It's worth studying. Maybe I can even have some fun with it..."

I'm hit with another jump-scare when the sound of heavy metal chains falls from all around me. As hard as it is to take my eyes off the wicked visage of Arthur Wilson, I need to make sure I'm not in any more danger from him and the spiders crawling around just above.

In the four bunk beds set into the wall, a wooden handle has appeared just above the pillow. Each handle hangs from a chain running up into the ceiling of the bunk bed.

A wave of grief washes over me when I notice one of the four beds is missing a handle. Clearly, it was meant for Chrissy. The lights flicker briefly, and by the time I look back to the gramophone, Wilson is gone.

Shiv pushes a handle and watches it swing on its chain. "So what is this, then? Now it's suddenly our turn to pull their chains? Why do I have a feeling this one is especially going to turn to shite?"

I sigh, knowing she's right, but we really have no choice. "It doesn't matter. Lucy has made it abundantly clear there's only one way we're getting out of here, and to do that, we have to play whatever sick game this is."

PQ stares up at the box of spiders, true fear turning him from the ultimate adventurer into a scared little boy. "Can I call dibs on a bottom bunk?" he asks, sitting down on the bed underneath the one that would have been Chrissy's.

"I'll take a top, if it's all the same." Shiv hops up onto the bunk above the one that's left for me.

I lie down, sure the next few minutes of my life will, at best, be extremely unpleasant. Whatever's about to happen, it's going to somehow involve spiders. My only consolation is I'm wearing a slightly oversized hoodie. While I prepare myself mentally, I'm able to also prepare myself physically. I pull the hood over my ears and crown, then yank the drawstring as tightly as I can until I'm looking as close to Kenny from *South Park* as possible. The way my hood feeds into the zipper of the jacket, it still leaves a portion of my mouth exposed, but I'll cross that bridge when I come to it. I then pull my hands into my sleeves, bunching up the cloth to keep as little flesh exposed as possible.

"One," Shiv calls out from the bunk above me.

I start taking deep breaths, like I'm about to be submerged underwater.

"Two," she says, a little later than I would have expected.

"Three!"

From above me, I hear her pull her chain. I do the same. It lowers about an inch and then abruptly stops. Nothing happens.

"Hey, PQ?" I call out, looking across the room at our third, who is in the bed opposite me.

He hiccups a whimper, then squeezes his eyes shut and pulls the handle.

A loud and irritating buzz, like something from a wrong answer on a game show, fills the room, and a wall of glass appears from some hidden compartment beneath me, sliding up and separating my inset bed from the rest of the room while still giving me a full view. My reaction is to release my hand from the chain and fight my way out of the bunk, but I force myself to stay in place to help my team. Somehow, I know this involves us holding on for as long as possible.

The buzzer finally stops, but the silence is replaced by what sounds like an ancient jet engine powering up. It's only then I notice a panel in the wood above me has slid open.

"Oh shit!" I understand what the mechanical sound is—there's a steady gust of air pressing down onto my chest.

I don't want to look, but I have to be sure. Our simultaneous pulling of the levers has powered up some sort of vacuum, and it's sucking the already angry spiders into tubes, then sending them hurtling at us through these holes in our bunks.

"Christ, kill me now," Shiv says, clearly understanding what's happening as well.

That's when the first spider drops onto me. Its tiny body skitters furiously across my torso, searching for either someplace to hide or something fleshy to take out its aggression on. I'm thankful for tucking my hoodie into my pants—it scrapes its tiny legs against the seam but finds no purchase.

Two more plop onto my stomach, quickly followed by another three. There's an itch inside my ear. Another on my heel. I know it's my mind playing tricks on me. There's no way they could be crawling in all those places. I saw all of them fall onto me. Felt them.

Didn't I?

A shiver runs down my body, and I squeeze my eyes shut, then turn my exposed nose and lips into the shoulder of my hoodie. They're crawling all over me, moving quickly. Another tingle dances across the back of my neck, A tickle creeps up my forearm. I can't tell what's real and what's a product of my own terror taking control of my synapses.

"Ow!" PQ calls from across the room. "Ow, hey!" From the sound of it, PQ is fighting the spiders, instead of trying to stay calm.

There's a little pinch on my ankle, just above my sock. I keep calm and pray that's the last bite as PQ continues his battle.

The pinch is now a throbbing pain that's only getting worse. I clench my jaw, the burning sensation running beneath my skin and into my body.

"Open your eyes," a voice whispers to me. I used to hear it so often, it might as well have been my own. It's the voice of my brother, Brian. "I can save you. Look at me."

*****

Ignore Brian. Keep your eyes closed. Turn to page 87.
Listen to your brother. Open your eyes. Turn to page 103.

I tap my finger several times on the library section of the map. "I think we should start here."

"Any reason why, besides the obvious?" Shiv's tone is defiant seemingly for defiance's sake.

"I'm just trying to think logically. We found his journal in the room where he chronicles his experiment specimens. His watch was in the room where he experimented on people who had taken opium. Wouldn't it make sense to you that he would keep his glasses in the place he reads books?"

"That's enough convincing for me," PQ mumbles, his voice slightly slurring. He presses his body and head against a wooden pole next to the check-in desk. It takes him noticeable effort to push himself off before he shuffles his way over to the staircase. "Let's get a move-on. I bet there's a comfy chair in there."

"Come on," I say, "let's help you upstairs." I reach my arm around him to take the role of leaning post, but he flinches at least six times when our bodies come into contact at different points. Once I have his arm over my shoulder and we're ready to go, he blows out a sigh of exhaustion, making me worry he may not even be able to make it to the library.

Slowly but steadily, we climb the stairs behind an impatient Shiv. She's holding the map, and once we reach the second floor, she leads us around a series of nonsensical twists and turns until we come upon a room with double doors and a tarnished bronze placard reading: "Library."

"Oh, thank the flying spaghetti monster," PQ wheezes, exhausted from the short trip.

Shiv pushes open the doors, revealing a modestly sized library, its walls lined with bookshelves crammed with dusty hardbacks. Hanging from its ceiling is a large crystal chandelier keeping this place more well-lit than almost any room we've seen so far. In one corner, I spot a large leather chair with an ottoman. It's the first stop PQ and I make. I take the time to set him down easy so as not to aggravate the dozens of bites spread across his body.

"All right, genius, what now?" Shiv asks, scanning the room for anything out of the ordinary.

Aside from the hundreds of books lining every inch of the walls, there are several comfy chairs, a large central table featuring several dozen books, and a few side tables hosting green-shaded lamps. I don't see a pair of spectacles or even a box which could contain something like that. The largest container in the entire room is an ink pot next to a piece of paper and quill pen on the corner of the center table.

*****

Look through the books on the main table.
Turn to page 142.
Scan the books along the walls for something that strikes
you. Turn to page 96.

"The bean what?" I ask, unable to understand her accent.

Her face turns cold in a snap, back to the Shiv I've come to know so far. She sneers at me. "A Banshee you arsehole. But if you're so eager, then go ahead already." Shiv juts her chin toward the hall.

"What? I'm just trying to understand what you said."

"Yeah, well, go have a look. If you come back alive, maybe we can have a chat."

I search for any cracks to try to get back into her good graces, but she's a wall. "Fine, I guess I'll be right back," I say, then step out into the passageway. Even though the door to the morgue is closed, the woman's weeping cuts through clearly, as if the door were nothing but a curtain. My heart races, and I pray the room is still locked when I reach for the handle.

It turns.

Damn.

I brace, ready to be hit with a blast of heat from the fire, but as I push the door open, it turns out smell is the more pressing matter. Chrissy's flesh, hair, and clothes were turned into barbeque by the fire, and all the associated odors were trapped, lingering in this room until just now. I'm halfway in before I have to turn around or risk heaving, staying in the entryway, where the smell of my cooked friend is diffused enough by stale basement air.

The ghostly figure, the "bean something," is down on her knees, sobbing over the black steaming husk of my former friend. I wonder if that's what my brother looked like in the end.

Probably not. He got buried in debris when our childhood home crumbled around him. It was most likely even worse.

Tears burn behind my eyes. Guilt pours into me, filling the void Chrissy has left behind. Unlike simply abandoning my brother, I had a direct hand in Chrissy's death. I pushed her away from my morgue container when she was desperately in need of help, didn't even give her a chance. There were at least a dozen other pods. Why did she have to try and pick mine?

A single hiccup of a sob escapes me, and I literally clasp my hands over my mouth, biting my lip to hold it back.

The woman takes her blood-soaked cloth and places it over the remains of Chrissy's face. A blue-white wisp lifts upward from the red cloth and into the sobbing woman's mouth. For once, she becomes silent, inhaling deeply. The mote of energy turns into a stream of ethereal stringy lights, crushing Chrissy's chest and causing her blackened skin to form a rippling web of cracks across her torso. There's a sound of shattering glass as her ribcage implodes. A round blue glow finishes out the stream of energy, and then Chrissy is nothing but a spent shell.

My hands do nothing to cover the sound when another sob escapes me. The weeping woman turns toward my direction, her cheeks gray and hollow. Her mouth is wide open and impossibly long, with a jawline running down twice the size of a normal face. It's a gaping hole, seemingly devoid of teeth, tongue, or any light that dare touch it. But what's most mesmerizing of all are her eyes, which are so bloodshot red they nearly glow. Beneath those eyes run wet streams of black mascara, carving asymmetrical lines down her face to her thin pointed nose.

And now, she is boring her bloodshot eyes into me.

I'm overcome with both sorrow and terror. It's like a magnet pulling me in two directions at once. Both feelings are mutually exclusive. I either want to break down into tears, to mourn my friend Chrissy, or scream and run as far and as fast as I can. To a degree, my choice ends up being made for me.

I can't help I've always been a sympathetic crier. Even if I wasn't standing over the remains of a person who had been one of my closest friends for the last two years, just being around someone else experiencing such a tangible expression of loss always cranks my emotions up to eleven. My eyes run, some of the strength sapped from my legs, and I lean into the doorframe of the morgue and cry.

The Banshee's puffy black dress turns from a mushroom cap on the floor to a thin stalk. She rises into the air and floats toward me, her eyes never wavering from mine and my fear pouring out with my tears. The Banshee meets me in the doorway, cocks her head to the side. Her ethereal, all-encompassing sobbing modulates, like a recording being altered in an editing program. It's like she's tuning her mourning to match the pitch and cadence of mine. She's learning how I cry...and finding a way to mirror it.

It isn't until every hiccup and sob is in sync that she pulls away from me, her white hair floating as if we are underwater. The Banshee bobs up in the air slightly, her form turning around, then drifts off down a hallway, crying my tears.

The further she floats from me, the calmer I feel. The Banshee's cry fades until there's only the low hum of electricity running across the lightbulbs overhead. I rub my wet eyes into my shoulder and sniffle up a bit of snot threatening to seep out of my nose. When I'm ready, I rejoin PQ and Shiv in the other room.

"Is she gone?" Shiv asks, trying to sound tough again. Her voice betrays her at the last second, quavering on her final syllable.

"Seems like, at least for now," I say. "What *was* that thing? And how did you know about it?"

Shiv's lips squeeze so tight they almost look like a puckered butthole, and she stares out into space. "Because I seen her. I was just a girl of seven, but I'll never go a day without being reminded of her. In Ireland, the Bean Sidhe is just as popular as your Big Foot. Only, we actually know she's real, yeah? We lived on a farm. Gran had been sick for nearly two years, wheezing all the time, nearly coughing up a lung. One night, she was making a God-awful racket. I was sleeping in the room next to hers, and out in the woods, I heard the sound of crying. I looked out my window, and that's when I saw her, feet half a foot off the grass, coming to my house."

As she's telling her story, PQ's eyes light up like it's Christmas. He lives to hear stories like this. "I can't believe you actually saw her. What did you do next?"

"I wanted to run and hide more than anything. I don't know why, but I just couldn't do it. She came right up to the house. I was sure she was after me. But then, she just vanished through the wall on the other side of mine. Into Gran's room."

"Did you follow her in?" PQ asks with rapt attention.

Shiv punches him in the arm. "Come on, I was seven, remember? I could barely even stand to listen to what was going on in there."

"And what *did* you hear?" he asks, rubbing the spot on his arm where Shiv just socked him.

"The Bean Sidhe wailed something fierce, so loud it easily drowned out all the hacking and choking sounds of my gran. Then after a while, it all got quiet, and the next thing I knew, I saw her floating back out of the house, headed back into the woods."

PQ grins. "Oooh, that gave me chills. Great story."

Shiv raises a fist. "I'm being serious here. You want another bruise to go with the one I just handed ya?"

"I'm good, sorry." PQ shakes his head and takes a step back from Shiv. "Don't hurt me, but I have to ask: what the hell is it doing here?"

It seems like the obvious question, and internally, I'm kicking myself for not asking sooner.

"This house is supposed to be haunted by the ghost of Arthur Wilson, one of the most famous serial killers in history, and yet so far, we've had a flaming morgue and a spirit of Irish legend. What gives?" he continues.

"It's gotta be the amulet, right?" I say, remembering our briefing and the crappy movie they made about this place ten years ago. "Didn't Lucy say it can tap into your worst fears, or something?"

Shiv presses her eyebrows together, like she's working out a math problem. "But how can that actually be true? I'm not denying that we're in some real shit here. We can all at least agree there's no such thing as ghosts or magic amulets, right?"

"We all filled out those questionnaires," PQ says. "They had a question asking about your worst fears. Did you by any chance write 'Banshees'?"

Shiv shakes her head, looking at PQ as if he were an alien. "What are ya, stupid? Why the hell would I actually give anyone that kind of ammunition, even for a game? I wrote 'bees.'"

"Are you scared of bees?" PQ asks.

"Of course not."

PQ turns to me. "What about you?"

"I wrote 'snakes,'" I say, then shake my head to indicate I also filled out a phony answer.

"And I'm just taking a stab in the dark here that you're afraid of fire?" While what Shiv says is a question, it sounds as if it were an accusation.

"I'd rather not say," I reply. It seems pretty obvious Shiv's got me figured out, but there's no way in hell I'm going to confirm it for them out loud. I never even told Chrissy about Brian.

"Well, this is concerning. Am I really the only one who filled out the form honestly?" PQ asks.

"It doesn't seem to matter. However they figured it out, it seems like they have us pegged anyway. If we have any hope of stopping this, we have to find those artifacts. What did Lucy say? Arthur's spectacles, journal, and pocket watch."

"I don't know," Shiv says. "I still think they're going to kill us either way."

"We have to try, or else Chrissy died for nothing." I shake my head, trying to convince myself as much as I am them. "I refuse to believe that our situation is completely hopeless. PQ, you still have those maps? Now that things seem at least somewhat quiet, maybe we can take a minute to actually look through them and figure out where we are."

PQ pulls the maps from his back pocket, then carefully unfolds each, making sure they don't tear across the fold lines. After a few seconds of studying the basement map, all we hear out of him is a simple yet concerning, "Huh."

"What is it?" I ask.

He points to a room on the map with the number four on it. On the map's right side is a legend citing room four as the morgue. However, the room we're in doesn't seem to correlate to the map in any meaningful way. "According to the map, the room we're currently in doesn't even exist," PQ says.

"Fat lot of help this is," Shiv mutters.

PQ nods. "Okay, true. This doesn't seem like it's one hundred percent accurate. But look, we've got the morgue here. If it's labeled, I'm guessing it's generally somewhere in the right area." He points to another room that just has a picture of a beaker inside. "I'm guessing there's some significance to this room. It's the only one on this floor with a picture instead of a name. Maybe that's the game's way of telling us where we'll find the first of Wilson's artifacts. The real question is, how do we get there? According to the map, the only path is to follow an intricate series of twists and turns that takes us all over this lower level. But again, reality and the map don't seem to line up. From where we are now, I can see a path that leads past the morgue that isn't even on the map. If we go that way, in general terms, it looks like a relatively straight shot to that room. We could potentially bypass almost the entirety of this maze. What do you guys think?"

Ignore the map. Take the shortcut. Turn to page 60.
Follow the map. Take the long way. Turn to page 39.

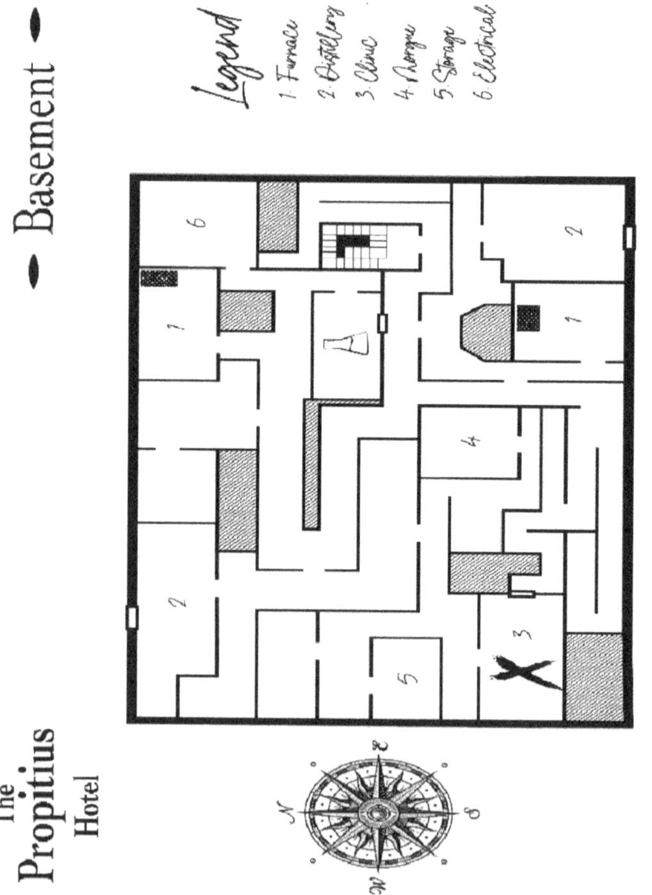

Shiv raises a good point, and if we have any hope of finding the secret passage Lucy escaped through, we're going to have to move sooner than later.

"Let's do it!" I call out, skipping a stair each time I pump my legs. I don't have to look back to know my companions follow closely behind, up the centennial staircase. The wood lets out a loud groan with each of their footfalls, giving me hope that maybe I can catch the sound of a rusty hinge swinging shut when I reach the landing.

On the second floor, there's a hallway to my left and an unmarked door to my immediate right. My first instinct is to sprint down the hallway, searching for clues; however, I'm glad I take a moment to examine the door before dismissing it as too obvious. There's a yellow light cutting a line across the bottom seam, brighter than any of the bulbs we've seen in this old hotel thus far. I also catch it not a moment too soon—the light switches off.

"They're behind that door!" Knowing it will be locked, I don't even bother with the knob. I throw the entire force of my weight behind the ball of my foot and kick the door several times by the latch. The door doesn't budge, but I don't let that stop me. After a few more kicks, the knob jiggles in place. Two more times, and there's a loud crack followed by the door flying inward.

The room is cramped and full of monitors, narrow passageways, and a hole in the center of the room, a ladder running in both directions. Squatting next to a computer is a skinny guy in a black shirt and matching sweatpants. His hair is a mess, and he looks familiar. I remember seeing him when I first entered Krentler Studios. He was the desk receptionist who told us to wait. I think his name is Todd.

"You're not supposed to be in here!" Todd's voice cracks, giving a feeble attempt at giving a command. "This is for crew only!"

All the fear I had of this hotel turns to rage at this grubby pissant watching us get tormented from behind the scenes. I want to grab the scrawny kid and wring his neck, but Shiv beats me to it. She shoves me aside, sprinting into the crew passage. Shiv makes it two steps in before there's a gleam of light and the sound of something thudding on the ground. Her momentum collapses, and her legs turn to jelly. I watch in shock as her body falls down the hole in the middle of the room.

I backpedal, but my foot bumps on something—Shiv's severed head.

From behind the door steps Arthur Wilson holding a now-bloodied axe and grinning like a lunatic.

Behind him, Lucy squeezes into view from one of the cramped hallways. "Todd, take a note."

"Yes, ma'am."

"Reinforce all the doors for the next batch."

Todd nods, typing on a tablet in his hands. "Got it."

Lucy turns her attention to me. "You just couldn't follow the rules, could you? And now look what's happened." She shakes her head in disappointment. "What a waste of a test group. Arthur, finish them off."

I try to retreat when Arthur approaches, but my foot slips on the blood oozing from Shiv's head, and I fall backward. I don't even have time to raise my arms before Wilson brings the blade of the axe swinging down into my face.

*****

The correct answer was to try and solve the riddle.
Turn to page 21.

"Get in!" I gesture wildly for Chrissy to abandon the occupied locker and squeeze into mine. It'll be a tight fit, but these things should be strong enough to hold two people at once. With the flames on the tile floor licking at her feet, Chrissy leaps into the body locker with me, and I waste no time trying to pull it shut.

Only, sliding us back into the wall isn't nearly as easy as pulling the locker out was. PQ and Shiv both seemed to slide themselves back in without issue. Between me franticly eyeing the immolating room and the smoke cutting visibility, I can't even tell which lockers they climbed into.

"What are you doing?" Chrissy asks with all the urgency in the world, lying back and watching me struggle to close us in.

"It's stuck. I can't get it to go back."

"Pull harder!" she demands. Chrissy then inches herself deeper into the small locker, as if that's going to make any sort of difference if I'm not able to get the damn thing shut.

I put some effort into jiggling the bed we're lying on, trying to loosen it. After a few solid shakes, the sound of a metal clack either means I've dislodged us from the metal runners, which would allow the locker to slide into the wall, or I've fixed something that got dislocated when Chrissy jumped onto the bed with me. I reach forward to the wall, pull as hard as I can, and thank my lucky stars when it finally starts to slide.

Not a moment too soon. The flames have made it across the room and are climbing the wall upon which we are perched.

I keep sliding us further, and further, toward safety. I'm almost there.

And then we stop.

With about six inches to go between the edge of the locker and the wall, the sound of metal on metal once again clinks, and we're not moving anymore. This time, there's no give when I try to rock us to the sides, no jiggling when I grab the ceiling and try to push. The locker is stuck where it is. There's no more planning, aside from just trying to make as much room as possible and hoping for the best.

"Slide down as far as you can," I tell Chrissy. "Curl up into a ball and cover your head."

The space isn't exactly roomy, especially with the two of us inside. Chrissy is able to hug her knees to her chest, but mine bang against the locker ceiling when I try to do the same.

A blast of heat rears up behind me. Though the flames haven't climbed enough to reach us yet, smoke billows in through the crack, causing us to choke and cough. They say smell is the strongest sense memory, and as the fire overtakes the room, it brings me right back to my bedroom, watching Brian burn.

Chrissy is screaming something, but I'm no longer paying attention to her. I pretend she's my brother, reach down, and grab hold of her as my hair catches fire. The heat and pain is unbearable, but at the same time, something about it feels right. This is how I was supposed to go ten years ago, back with my brother in our old house.

*****

The correct answer was to shut myself in alone.
Turn to page 109.

I can't afford to open my eyes, never mind untuck my face from the deep corners of my armpit. The tentative seal between the edge of my hood and my arm is an imperfect dam where dozens of arachnids are probing for a tiny crack in which to insinuate themselves. The thrumming pain in my leg is now pulsing along with the *thump-thump* of my heart, and my body is trying to send everything it can to defend against the corrosive toxin seeping into my ankle.

Though I can no longer check-in visually with PQ, I'm forced to listen to his panicked struggle against the army of tiny nightmares. His hyper-aggressive approach to dealing with the infestation doesn't seem to be going very well. Between the reactive yips and yowls to what I assume to be many bites, he frequently punctuates his agony with vindictive cries of success.

"Take that, you little S-O-Bitch!" he shouts, in the midst of what sound like pointless victories.

"I can help you." A competing voice rises above PQ's cries and my own mental whirlwind of panic. "Just open your eyes," the ghost of my brother whispers so closely, I can feel hot air against my ear, even through the fabric of the hood.

Once again, I fight to push him away, redoubling my efforts to keep my eyes closed and jaw shut. The more I remain perfectly still, the less frantic the spiders in my pod seem to be. What started out as a mad dash to squeeze into any conceivable gap in my clothes has slowed to methodical probing for weak spots in my defenses.

Unfortunately, I have two massive holes in my makeshift protective suit, and one by one, the spiders seem to be finding the cool dark gap lying between my socks and pants. Tiny legs tap hesitantly around my unbitten left ankle and slowly start to climb inside. It's funny, my right leg feels like it is practically on fire, yet on my left side, the tickling sensation of tiny legs against the hairs on my shin are almost just as unbearable.

In my mind, two camps form. One screams at me to breathe through this and just continue to remain perfectly still for as long as possible. The other is urging me, with every ounce of adrenaline it can muster, to slide the arch of my right shoe down my left pant leg as hard as possible, hopefully squishing the spiders before they climb high enough to reach some of the more tender areas.

Both sides are spinning compelling arguments around and around in my head. I'm just about to give in and start scraping at my leg when chains jingle across the room, followed by a mechanical hiss. The air pressure bearing down on my chest from the vacuum is gone, despite the fact the suction sound has gotten louder.

Maybe I'm distracted by the grating noise, but I can't feel any spiders on me anymore either. The pain in my leg still aches like nobody's business, but all the creepy crawling up my legs, across my torso and face, it's all gone. It's only now that I dare to open my eyes and hazard a glance around me. Firstly—and just as I expected—my brother's burnt spirit is nowhere to be seen, confirming he was either a figment of my imagination or, what's much more likely, a manifestation of the house.

PQ's bunk confirms my suspicions—this was a test of endurance. Releasing his handle seems to have shut off the flow to Shiv's bunk and mine and redirected the entire colony of brown recluses into PQ's pod. He's flailing wildly to smash and squish every spider he can, but his body is covered in the little monsters scurrying at speeds so fast, it's hard to even keep my eyes focused on a single body at a time. I look up at the glass box on the ceiling with the pocket watch and count ten spiders, still clinging to their cage, slowly get hoovered up and sent directly to PQ. The spiders fight against the current, but their effort is in vain. Their number dwindles to five, four, and eventually a lone soldier. It's only when that last recluse disappears into the pneumatic system hidden in the walls that another blaring buzz fills the room.

The glass wall keeping me in the bunk slides away, and I leap to my feet, brushing off any eight-legged hitchhikers. Nothing falls to the floor. I double-check my bunk and am surprised I can't even find a single spider remaining, alive or dead.

The glass bottom of the box on the ceiling drops out at the same time as the wall holding PQ in his bunk, and both come tumbling to the floor.

"Get them off!" PQ screams, rolling out of the bed and onto the floor.

I rush to his side, and aside from seeing a man covered in growing red welts, I can't find a single spider on him.

"They're gone. It's over now," I say, though he doesn't seem to hear me.

He continuously rolls around, slapping his palms against random parts of his body.

"Hey, PQ, calm down."

Slowly, PQ comes to the realization that, just like in my pod, all the spiders have disappeared. Also, just like me, there isn't a single body to be found.

Behind me, I hear the thud of heavy boots landing on the ground. "Who else feels like they need a shower after that?" Shiv's face is stony, and she bends over and picks up the tarnished brass pocket watch from the floor.

"Shiv, are you okay? I couldn't hear you through that whole thing." I look her up and down for bite marks or swelling. Despite the fact she has her arms and head completely exposed, she seems unharmed.

She shrugs. "Just cupped a hand over my mouth and nose and held perfectly still. As long as I didn't move, it didn't really seem like they gave two shits about me. I'm fine, aside from being a bit icked out. How did you two fare?" she asks, though her voice loses some of its bravado when she begins to notice PQ is absolutely covered in welts.

I lift a pant leg, revealing what turns out to be a single red bump just above my sock line. Considering the level of pain my leg is in, I'm a little shocked to discover I only have a single bite. PQ lets out a moan from the ground. Given how much my single bite hurts, I can hardly even imagine how much worse it must be for him.

"Christ, PQ, what the hell happened to you?"

"I told you, I don't like spiders," he groans.

"So, erm, where did all the spiders go?" Shiv asks.

"I don't think they were real," I reply.

"This feels pretty real to me." PQ slowly pushes himself to his hands and knees, hissing in pain each time his swelling skin comes into contact with the floor.

"Maybe *real* isn't the right word."

"If you're about to tell me I just got attacked by a swarm of ghost spiders, I'm calling it quits right here."

This time, I take a second to collect my thoughts before answering. "Not ghost spiders either. I think they're manifestations Arthur is conjuring with that amulet. They're real for as long as Arthur wants them to be. I think it's becoming increasingly apparent that either Arthur Wilson or Krentler Media knows what scares us the most and is using the Amulet of Duriel to temporarily conjure up our worst fears and give them form."

Shiv nods, working through the thought exercise with her razor-thin eyebrows pressed together. "Clearly, the spiders were here for PQ, and you all know my feelings on the Banshee. Here's my question...What's your fear, Jeremy?"

"You already guessed it, remember?" I said, which isn't a total lie. "I don't like fire. But we already faced that in the morgue."

"But Lucy...She said the fire was already planned when we talked to her in the lobby. Are you saying it's just a coincidence that your fear lines up with something they already had planned?"

I shrug, trying to play it off. "It seems like they set this whole place up with spiders in advance. I don't know what to tell you."

Shiv interrogates me with her eyes. I make sure not to blink. Finally, she nods.

"So, in that case, do you think each of these phobia manifestations are, like, a one-time thing? Like a one and done?" Shiv sounds more unnerved at the thought of her Banshee returning than she did during the entire episode with the spiders.

"I sure hope so," PQ says, finally on his feet but heavily relying on a wall to support his weight.

I don't have the heart to tell them I omitted an important detail regarding my fear of fire and that the charred, melted spirit of my dead brother has been following me around since we got here. Instead, I try to redirect the conversation and keep us all moving forward. "One thing's for sure, something in this house will definitely kill us all if we can't find that last artifact and then destroy Arthur and his amulet. We gotta focus on pushing forward."

By the time I've finished talking, PQ has already limped over to the staircase ladder and is gently trying to pull himself up. "You don't have to tell me twice. I need to get out of this room, like, yesterday."

Five minutes later, we're back in the lobby, and once again, a nearly blinding purple arc of lightning crackles within the Ectoplasmic Containment Unit when Shiv drops Arthur's pocket watch inside.

"Can we sit for a minute?" PQ gasps, clearly out of breath just from the journey here. He's panting, sweaty, and every minute or so, he has a small tremor twitching through his whole body.

"That's a good idea," I say, trying to keep spirits up. It also helps to mask the fact I have absolutely no idea what to do next. Unless Lucy shows up with another hint, or we take another pass at the maps, I'm completely clueless as to what the next step should be. The idea of trying to find a pair of glasses in this hotel without clear directions feels like trying to find a needle in a haunted haystack full of traps straight out of a *Saw* movie.

To take PQ's mind off the pain, we have him pull out the map, each of us taking one floor and scouring it for clues for what to do next. There are three pages to the map, giving half-cooked blueprints for the basement, first, and second floor. I'm handed the second-floor map, which is a space we haven't even explored yet.

Two rooms pique my interest when I read the key on the side of the page. On one hand, there's a library listed in the dead center of the second floor. If I were a pair of spectacles, what more appropriate place than that? If his journal was in the room where he kept his specimens and his pocket watch was in the den where he just had to wait for people to get high before snatching them, why wouldn't he keep his glasses in the library?

A second room on the map's key pops out to me for an entirely different reason. There's apparently an apothecary on the second floor. I know it's a stretch, but there's a chance we could find something in there to ease PQ's pain.

*****

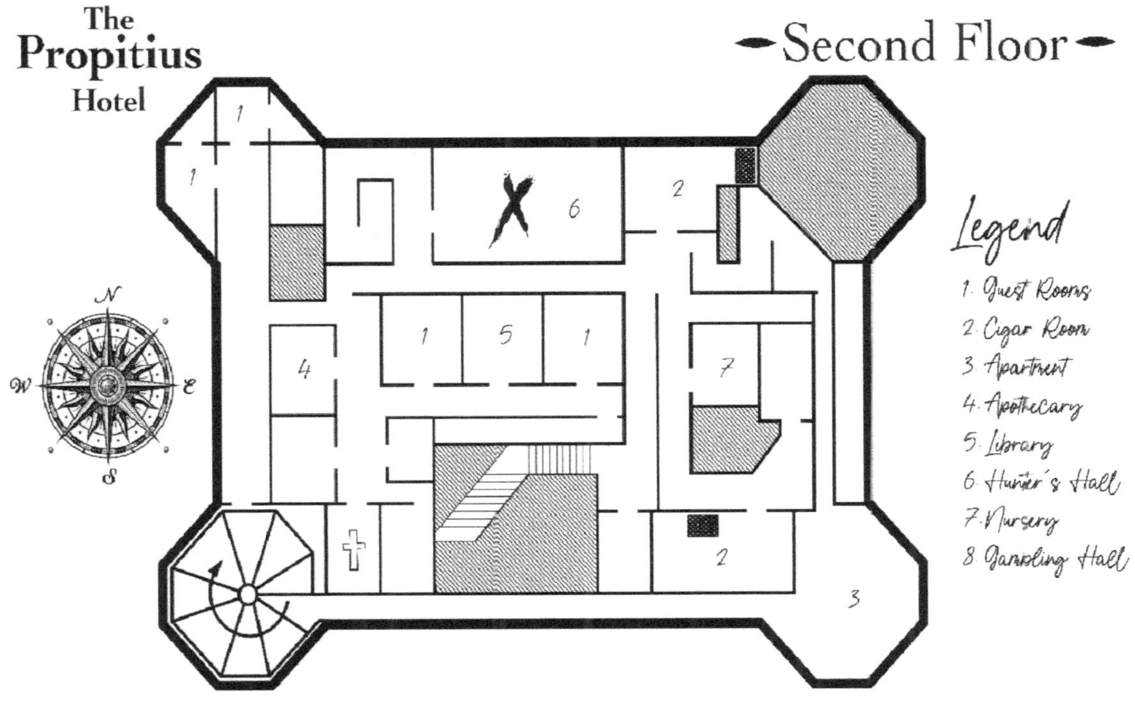

Suggest the library. Turn to page 74.
Suggest the apothecary. Turn to page 10.

There's something contagious about Shiv's bottomless pit of rage. She hurls herself at the seemingly unarmed specter, and I back her up, no more than a step behind. This way, I'm only a half-second later than her in seeing her fate and realizing mine is both imminent and unavoidable.

To both of our credits, it was incredibly easy to miss the fact Arthur was standing on nothing but air. One moment, Shiv is in front of me, winding up her fist for a punch. The next, she's screaming and falling into a black abyss. I've already got too much momentum. There's no chance of slowing before I follow suit. I plummet down the trap door and find myself flying along another pitch-black slide. However, unlike the last, when this one lets out, I can't help but deliver a pair of feet straight into Shiv's face.

She curses when my heel connects with her cheek, though I choose to believe she's swearing more at the situation than at me. As far as I can tell, the two of us are in an oversized metallic egg of some sort. The only light I can see is a reddish glow percolating under a metal grate floor. I try to take a few deep breaths to catch my bearings, but when I inhale, my lungs burn from the intense humidity, and sweat beads across my brow.

"You shouldn't have done that," another voice says, joining Shiv and me in the cramped metal room.

"Christ, what the hell is that?" Shiv wails with pure terror, pointing directly behind me.

There's a flare-up of heat and no need for me to turn around to explain. "Shiv, I'd like you to meet my brother, Brian. He died in a house fire when we were kids."

"Well, what the hell is *he* doing here?" she asks.

I try to soften my face and give her a sympathetic look, but instead, I feel like all I can muster is a wince of regret. "If I had to guess, I think he's here to finish what began when we were kids."

Shiv shakes her head. The light below us brightens, revealing a flame just under the grate, licking at our feet. "I'm not in the mood for riddles, Jeremy. What the hell is happening?"

I scan my eyes around the metal egg, noticing the passage we fell through has sealed off completely, leaving only one small pipe at the very top to vent smoke. With a nod of my head, I feel strangely at peace. "I'm no expert, but I'm pretty sure we're in the crematorium."

"The *what?*" she asks. "How are you sitting there so calm? We have to get out of here!"

The heat beneath us surges again. Now I can see fire peeking above the mesh. Shiv pounds at the metal walls but lets out a shriek of pain when the flesh on the bottom of her fist fuses with the steel walls. She rips her hand away, and strings of flesh pull away with it, like it was made of taffy.

My eyes sting, sweat dripping. I close them. It's for the best. I try to block out the sounds of Shiv's desperation.

Brian's small hand reaches out and grabs mine. I squeeze it tightly, the heat growing to a nearly unbearable level. The fire joins our hands together as flesh melts into flesh.

*****

The correct answer was to stop Shiv from attacking Arthur.
Turn to page 69.

"I bet one of these books is, like, the knob to a secret door or something." I step up to a wall and examine the book spines. This section seems to be mostly about mining—its history, techniques, memoirs from pioneers and magnates. None of them seem to strike me as particularly interesting, or relevant to what we've experienced thus far, so I keep on moving.

"This is seriously your plan?" Shiv says in a way clearly intended to make me sound dumb. "Let's just look at all the books in this entire library until we get lucky or realize we're not even in the right room?"

Frustration rises in my chest, though I'm not sure if it's because Shiv's being antagonistic or if it's because she's making a valid point. I don't care. I double down. "This place is begging to have a trick door somewhere in the room. I'm not saying read the title of every single book or anything. Just keep an eye out for something that looks like it could be out of place."

I scan another section of the library. This shelf is full of medical textbooks describing procedures and diagnoses I'm sure are outdated by nearly a century. I keep an eye out for books of irregular shape, size, or with text a font just a little too crisp to belong with these old tomes. A few books feel like they could stand out, but nothing special happens when I try to pull them from the rack.

By the time I reach the third bookshelf, my eyes are glazing over. All the adrenaline and constant energy exertion is finally catching up to me, and I'm losing steam fast. The next shelf of books takes me more than twice as long as the last, with me going back and starting over several times because my mind wanders.

After about ten minutes of searching, Shiv lets out a sigh of displeasure. "I never thought I'd say this in here, but my God, am I bored."

As if on cue, an entire bookshelf suddenly swings open, just like the door I suspected would lie somewhere in the room.

"I couldn't agree with you more." Lucy strides into the library.

This time, she's accompanied by a woman in her mid-forties wearing a black jumpsuit. Her hair matches her outfit, and her pale face is punctuated by firetruck-red lipstick. However, the detail that currently has my attention is the pistol she's gripping in her hand.

"You guys," Lucy says, shaking her head. "I'm sorry to say this, but you are being so agonizingly boring. If this really were being televised right now, do you think an audience would want to stick around and watch you look at every single book in this entire library?"

A cocktail of rage and fear bubbles inside me. I want to curse her out, to spit every obscenity I can imagine her way, but I bite my tongue. She holds all the cards, and despite my intense desires to air my grievances, I have a strong feeling it will end in my imminent demise.

Meanwhile, Lucy continues to berate us. "Seriously, you guys, we put a whole pile of books on the table in the middle of the room for a reason. You didn't think to start there? Instead, you looked at this small, curated collection and thought, 'Hmm, let's ignore this obvious clue and just wander around with our thumbs up our buttholes for a while.'"

She points at PQ, who seems like he's barely even conscious at this point.

"I mean, look at this guy on the couch. He's definitely going to kick the bucket soon, but at least he gave it his best effort. You, on the other hand, Jeremy, have been a huge disappointment. You seemed so smart earlier. What happened?"

"We're all just doing our best here. It's not our fault that every single aspect of this place is another difficult puzzle. We're hurt, we're exhausted, scared. It's all too much."

We stare each other down, and for a moment, I'm wondering if Lucy will just have me shot now. However, a slow smile creeps across her lips.

"You know what? You're absolutely right. I know you may think we're just putting you through this for some twisted pleasure, but in reality, we have five different departments taking copious notes on every conversation, every decision, hell, even every fart you make. It's all valuable data, and believe me, based on your performance, we will *definitely* be making some major revisions to the competition for our next batch of beta testers."

Lucy begins to turn and venture back into the hidden door, when Shiv calls out to her again. "What, so you're just going to leave us in here after that? No calling up your ghost lap dog to chop us up?"

With a condescending laugh and a quick shake of her head, Lucy explains, "After how badly you just fumbled this puzzle, it's not even worth the effort." She looks over to the armed woman next to her and nods. "Charlotte?"

The raven-haired woman, presumably Charlotte, returns the nod. The room explodes with sound as she fires her gun. A red hole appears between Shiv's eyes, and the books on the wall behind her are coated in a splatter of blood and little chunks of brain and skull.

Charlotte turns to me. "Sorry, kid, you blew it." She aims the pistol's barrel at me.

There's another explosion and a flash of light.

*****

The correct answer was to examine the books on the table.
Turn to page 142.

I thought I had tortured myself long enough for Brian's death. But now, I realize no matter what I do, I will never have a clear conscience.

"Please, Jeremy, I don't have long!" Even through all the burns and the deformities, his agony and fear are palpable. His hand is outstretched as far as his little arm will reach. Flesh drips from his burning bones, like wax to the floor.

I wonder if he actually feels it—if he's been actively feeling this constant suffering ever since I entered the hotel.

After one last shuddering breath, I reach out and take his burning hand in mine. The pain is instant and all-consuming. An impossible heat bears down on me, piercing through my skin and muscles, cooking my organs, charring my bones. The little hand is stronger than I expected and yanks me into the circle of fire.

Up close, Brian's face has changed. He now reports a twisted glee no child—especially not Brian—could ever conjure. His screams turn into a malicious giggle, his teeth yellow and crooked like Wilson's.

I try to pull away, but it's far too late. I burn while the monstrous spirit sucks me into his house.

*****

The correct answer was to leave Brian. Turn to page 153.

I only have a small window to capitalize on Arthur's distraction. We've come so far, and I can't end this without Shiv's help. Staying low, I sprint up the stairs and snatch Shiv's wooden stake from the floor. I'm coming at him from behind, and if I were dealing with a creature from the reality I lived in yesterday, I would have just clubbed him over the head, or tried to stab him in the back with the nasty point.

But this is not the reality I know, and I have a strong feeling that if I try to attack Arthur directly in this state, there's a good chance I'll simply pass right through him versus actually hit him.

That's when something hits me.

His body may be incorporeal, but the injuries we have sustained from his weapons so far have all been real.

I grip the chair's leg in two hands, holding it out in front of me in the pathway Arthur seems to be preparing to slash with his bone saw. Just as I suspected, I pass right through him. However, it's the wooden leg that suffers the bone saw's strike instead of Shiv's face. The teeth of the saw get caught in the wood's grain, and again, I find myself catching Arthur by surprise.

I pull the leg downward with all my might, and the bone saw slips away from his spectral hand. As if I were a football player receiving the ball, I keep going, continuing to run down the hall. Now that I have his weapon, I've definitely earned Wilson's attention.

"Shiv! Get the spectacles in the box while I distract him!" I run a few more steps, afraid to look behind me and find Arthur close on my tail. However, when I don't hear any sort of response, worry overtakes me, and I finally turn to see what's happening on the balcony.

She's face down on the floor, arm outstretched within half an inch of the spectacles. One simple push and they would fall right into the box. But she's not moving, and

Arthur is standing over her body, sporting his grin that makes my stomach turn. Sticking out of Shiv's back is a glint of light—a scalpel plunged straight into her spine.

"Shiv?" I ask.

"Run," she gasps.

My heart drops. Shiv doesn't deserve to die alone. I did everything I could to save her, but in the end, I'm just one helpless college student up against an entire corporation using ghosts to do their dirty work. It almost feels ludicrous that I'm still trying to find a way to survive this, when I know how high the odds are stacked against me. It's not like they're just going to let me walk out of here, even if I do manage to stop Wilson and destroy his amulet.

Despite my despair, my legs carry me back toward the bowels of the house.

Arthur reaches into his sleeve, pulls out another scalpel. I turn and run down the hallway. No plan, no ideas, no hope. Just following Shiv's last word: run.

I hurry around the corner. There's a brief flicker of lights and then a sudden and intense pain in my shoulder when I run headfirst into Arthur and his blade, which is buried at least three inches.

Wilson's already got another scalpel in hand and looks like he's sizing me up, deciding where to stick the next one. The corners of his lips curl up, and he slashes the scalpel across my face. It's shallow, but I feel the blade's bite, and blood runs down my jaw. I back away until my body presses against a corner.

There's nothing left in me. Even if I were to defend against one of his attacks with the bone saw I stole, he would just have another scalpel ready and waiting for me.

I let out a long breath, feeling a resolute blanket of acceptance drape over me. Yes, I know my fate. Deep down, I've known my fate from the moment we got here.

I spread my arms, opening myself, allowing Wilson carte blanche to finish me however he wishes. Part of me was hoping that by giving up, I would make his kill bittersweet, but the lustful glee on his face doesn't seem any less intense than any other time I've seen him in here. Slowly, as if to confirm I'm at his mercy, he raises his scalpel to my throat. He presses it gently at first, letting my skin do the work of tearing itself under the pressure of the blade rather than carving into me himself. Just when the first rivulet of blood trickles down my neck, he pulls away.

Yet *another* cruel game.

But then he doubles over, and his mouth turns into a deep frown. Purple lightning dances around his body, and for once, it's Wilson's turn to be afraid.

I realize what's happened.

Shiv just used what little lifeforce she had left to push the glasses over the edge of the balcony and into the box, meaning...

Meaning Wilson is now *vulnerable.*

*****

Go for the throat. Turn to page 138.
Go for the amulet. Turn to page 167.

I do as the voice says, lifting my head from my shoulder and opening my eyes. My dead brother's burnt and blistered face is inches away. His skin has melted to the point he no longer has anything resembling a nose or lips, and his eyelids are gone entirely.

I rear my head back on instinct, and it squishes something against the glass. A scream claws its way out of my mouth, and just like that, several spiders claw their way in. I shut my mouth, try to shove their bodies to the sides of my tongue, to masticate the little bastards to death. But it's too hard to tell what's going on between the frantic poking of dozens of legs and pinching fangs against my cheeks. I gag when a tiny body squeezes down my throat, biting me all the way.

I let go of the handle.

I don't mean to, but I need both hands to swat at the second wave of spiders sprinting up my body and vanishing between the now-loosened seam of my hoodie and my skin. Swatting at my face, my ears, I rake my hands across my head. I pull off my hood, now convinced there are more spiders inside of it than out. Letting my hands out of their sleeves, I pinch the zipper between two fingers. As I pull it down, at least a dozen spiders land on top of my hand and sink their fangs into my soft skin.

It's becoming difficult to swallow. My tongue is swelling up, and so is my throat. No, not just swelling. Corroding. The venom is eating away at my mouth and esophagus. To compensate, my body is fighting it with inflammation. Either one is sure to kill me. At this point, it's just a question of which will get me first.

Pain takes over every nerve ending of my body, and my breathing becomes increasingly difficult. I shift my eyes back to the burnt husk of my brother, swearing I can feel his heat. He reaches his arm around me, pulling me close to him.

"It's okay, brother. I have you."

*****

The correct answer was to ignore Brian. Turn to page 87.

"We have to get out of here." Shiv's voice cracks in terror.

"No," I say, fighting against my own fight-or-flight reaction telling me I need to get as far away from here as possible.

"What do you mean, no?" Shiv asks, sounding insulted. "She killed my gran. She's come after us before. Trust me, we want to be far away when she gets here."

I shake my head. "I'm sorry, but you're wrong. I know why the wailing woman is coming. It's not for us."

My whole body shivers when a woman in a black dress passes through the wall, hovering nearly a foot off the floor. Her face is covered in white hair, and in her hand, she holds a white bloody cloth. Just as I suspected, she's not heading for us. Instead, she's moving toward the now-lifeless body of my friend. Her sobs echo around the room, dripping with a sadness that makes my heart ache and my chest heave.

"Oh my God." Shiv's voice wavers on the verge of tears.

Three more forms float into the library behind the Banshee. First comes Chrissy looking how I always knew her, with the exception her eyes have become nothing more than white shining orbs. Behind her is my little brother, Brian, still wearing the same *SpongeBob* pajamas from the night of the fire. I want him to notice me, to see some trace of humanity in my little brother, but I might as well be invisible to him. The third, and final, apparition in the Banshee's tow is an elderly woman dressed in a blue nightgown.

"Gran?" Shiv says, followed by a hiccup. "Gran, it's me. It's Shiobhan."

The ghosts don't look our way. They don't even seem to notice anything but the Banshee. Their faces are all slack, in a completely neutral look reading of nothing but emptiness. They make their way to the Banshee, only separating to form a square around PQ's desecrated body.

My eyes sting, and tears roll down my cheeks. My brother looks so alive but so hollow. I want to see PQ again, free from the spreading sores from the spider bites, without the fountains of blood from being impaled by glass. But at the same time, I feel immense sadness at the thought of seeing his old form robbed of all the smiles and proud weirdness that made PQ who he was.

The Banshee bends over him and presses the bloody cloth to his mouth. His body surges, as if a doctor has just run defibrillators across his chest. He sinks into the chair then, the Banshee sucking blue wisps of energy from his mouth. His slightly round belly shrinks until he's skinnier than Chrissy, his lungs snapping when they get sucked in as well.

A new form joins the group of spirits. Just as I suspected, PQ's eyes are blank white, and his face shows a complete lack of expression, depriving him of everything that once made him unique. For a second, I think he looks over to me, but it could just be a trick of the light when he turns to face the Banshee and her cadre of souls. Without delay, the group floats back across the library the way they came, each disappearing behind the wall until there is nothing but the sound of Shiv and me crying.

Once we have collected ourselves, I notice something else where we placed all the required books before. The entire panel has shifted, and sitting on top of a small display are a pair of round spectacles. I wipe my face against my sleeve, climb to my feet, and grab Arthur Wilson's glasses.

"You ready to finish this?"

Shiv looks back at the wall of books, where both of us had just been so close yet so far away from our loved ones. She lets out one last sniffle, then nods. "Let's go."

What should be a quick walk back to the lobby ends up taking ages. The two of us, exhausted and wounded, limp one step closer toward the finish line. We freeze at the top of the stairs and stare at a figure standing in the lobby between us and the Ecto-whatever box. He's mostly a silhouette against the rainbow of colored light seeping in through the lobby's stained glass windows; however, his bright white eyes sparkle in the shadow of his face.

It's totally unlike the looks on the spirits of our family and friends—their eyes and faces resembled cheap replica masks of the people they once were. The spirit of Arthur Wilson, on the other hand, is every ounce as gleefully malicious as he was in life.

"Christ on a cracker," Shiv says. "Are they being serious with us right now?"

A smile full of crooked and rotten teeth spreads across Wilson's lips, and he steps forward, bringing his face into the pale light of the lobby's chandelier—something I'm intent on steering far away from. The way Arthur's foot moves forward is completely unnatural. It's almost as if he were walking backward on film and then the tape was reversed.

Step by reverse-backward step, he silently approaches the stairs. He never breaks eye contact with me, though given his pure-white eyeballs, I can almost guarantee Shiv probably feels like he's staring at her as well. There's one other thing I notice shining in the reflection of the chandelier's light. He's wearing a gold chain necklace with a ruby-red gem at the center of a gold pendant.

It must be the Amulet of Duriel, the artifact that's been bringing all our nightmares to life.

Somehow, we have to get past Arthur and drop his spectacles in the box, which will make him vulnerable, if Lucy wasn't lying. Even then, despite our rather serious wounds, Shiv and I are expected to somehow overpower this undead psychopath and destroy his amulet once and for all.

"All right, Jeremy," Shiv whispers, slowly limping backward. "This time, I am asking for your advice. What do we do?"

*****

Toss the spectacles at the Ectoplasmic Containment Unit.
Turn to page 30.
Split up. Turn to page 170.

Chrissy keeps screaming, but I've already slid myself into the locker and felt a latch click shut. Another worry immediately pops up in my head, wondering how the hell I'm going to get out of here now that I'm locked in. There's no other doors or hinges from inside. Considering the locker's purpose, it makes sense why.

"Help me, Jeremy! It burns!"

In the complete and total darkness of my makeshift coffin, Chrissy's cries for help sound even more distressing. I regret shutting myself in and claw uselessly at the head of the drawer.

"Chrissy, you need to find another locker, *now*!" I shout, feeling helpless as I tell her the obvious. My own voice reverberates around this small metal space and bounces back into my ears at twice the volume I thought I projected, and my eardrums throb.

I pray the next sounds I hear are her opening another drawer and quickly shutting it. Given prayer has never helped me before, I shouldn't be surprised when it fails me now. Instead of just opening another locker, she just keeps banging.

"Let me in! Somebody let me in!" she wails through tears of panic.

"Fuck off and find your own," Shiv calls out in a tinny voice from inside her locker.

Chrissy's begging for help turns into screams of pain. My lungs heave in my chest, and I flashback to my brother burning up while I'm cloistered away, completely helpless to do anything about it.

There's a click just behind my head. An unbelievable wave of heat blasts me in the face. The perfect seal to my locker is broken, and Chrissy starts to pull me out.

Only it's not Chrissy standing above me. At least, not the Chrissy I knew. The figure looming over my locker is bright red, the skin of her face blistering and peeling away.

Whatever hair she had left smolders and glows between chunks of crispy black char all over her now-bald head. Her eyes are transfixed on mine. She doesn't blink, though I'm not sure she even has eyelids anymore to perform that function.

It's horrifying and heartbreaking to see one of my best friends in this condition. For a moment, I want to just sit here and burn too.

But I can't. I have to survive. For my family. For the memory of my brother.

And so, in order to survive, I do what is maybe the worst thing I've ever done.

I fight.

Chrissy's bony black fingers are yanking at the drawer, attempting to pull it open, and every time I try to push her hands away, she comes back at me, even more frantic. My instincts take over; survival is all that matters. I punch her hands, feeling her cooked flesh smoosh under my knuckles, and strike at anything separating me from closing the door. Bones crack and crunch under mine, and I continue to smash my hand against her fragile digits. When she finally pulls away, I grab the ceiling of the morgue locker and slam myself back in as hard as I can.

Chrissy's already unbearable wails reach a new pitch. In the blackness, what feels like several small charred hot dogs fall onto my face, and I realize they are Chrissy's fingers.

The dying screams of my good friend slowly peter out, and I try not to vomit all over the severed fingers trapped in this tiny metal coffin with me. Eventually, the fire dies down, and there's only one sound reverberating in the darkness. The sound of my own hiccupping breath is horrific, but I would give anything to hear Chrissy screaming again. It would at least mean she's still alive.

Claustrophobia begins to set in, and my breathing in this shallow box rasps heavy in my ears. I press my hands against the edge of the drawer by my head. It's hot to the touch, but there's a stillness to it leading me to believe the fire in the morgue has been extinguished. I run my hands against the darkness, hoping I somehow missed a latch or knob somewhere before, but the metal is smooth. My breath grows louder, and my fears mount. I can't think beyond how loud my breath is. It's all I can focus on, and it's driving me crazy. If I don't get out of this death box soon, I worry I'll asphyxiate and...

The metal wall down by my feet drops open, and my eyes adjust to a dim orange glow beyond my pod. I squirm my way out, feetfirst. I've barely made it onto the hard-packed dirt of a dingy brick-walled room, when I'm assaulted by a figure and thrown into a wall.

"Jesus H. Christ, guy. What the hell is wrong with you?" Shiv presses her forearm into my windpipe, pinning me to the bricks and forcing me to gasp for breath. "Why didn't you tell us that was going to happen?"

I try to speak, but all I can choke out is, "Help!" I'm not a small guy by any means, but my legs are already trembling from listening to my friend burn. Even if I did have the nerve, Shiv is incredibly strong and built like a biker. Behind her, PQ looks at us with confusion.

"PQ, help," I whisper, this time reaching out for him, even though he's across the room.

Shiv doubles down on her chokehold and presses me even harder into the wall. My pulse pounds in my temple, and white stars dance around the periphery of my vision.

"Hang on," PQ says, putting a hand on Shiv's shoulder.

She snaps her head toward him, narrowing her eyes. After a second, she nods, then releases the pressure from me and takes a measured step back.

Left to support my own weight, I collapse to the ground when my legs give out, not sure if it's the prolonged lack of oxygen or a response to Chrissy's death.

"I didn't know," I say, tears streaming down my cheeks. "I don't know this would happen, I swear."

"Then this is all just a big trick? We were led to think we're testing some horror competition, but it must really be a hidden prank show, and we're already on it?" Shiv says.

I shake my head. "It's not a trick! I saw her burn!"

Shiv swipes a dismissive hand at me. "Eh, that sounds like something someone in on all of this would say. I'm sorry, but you're gonna have to do more than that to convince me."

A flash of anger gets me back on my feet. I stomp across the room and lean into my old morgue coffin, grabbing a handful of Chrissy's burnt, severed fingers. After throwing the charred bloody stumps at Shiv's face, I am slightly satisfied to see one leave a black and red smear across her cheek.

"What do you think *these* are, then?" I shout at her. "Pigs in a blanket?"

She bends over and takes a second to examine them closely. Upon realizing what they actually are, she rears her head back in disgust. "Ugh! What the actual fuck!"

"Still look fake to you?" I bark.

"So what the hell is this? An actual reality show where you snuff it if you fail? You Americans and your garbage reality TV. Is there anything you won't do?"

"No," PQ says simply. "Actually, this kind of feels like the natural progression of things. Remember that show *Moment of Truth*, where they hooked up people to lie detectors on national TV and would ask them things, like if they ever cheated on their spouses? People ruined their marriages, admitted to crimes, all sorts of stuff. And that was, like, fifteen years ago. *Survivor* has consistently been in the top ten ratings since it premiered over twenty years ago, and the episodes where people have to get emergency evacuations often get the most viewers. I mean, heck, have you turned on TLC lately? Or some of the programming from our lovely hosts at Krentler Media? Factor in all the fictionalized versions of this exact kind of thing—*Running Man, Battle Royal, Hunger Games*, even a couple of the *Saw* movies. And don't even get me started on our current political climate. I *absolutely* think America is ready to watch people die on live TV."

"But how can they think they're going to get away with this? Christ, they're going to kill us down here."

"I think that's mostly where our modern politics comes in," PQ says regretfully. "Don't forget that Krentler Media started out as an alt-right 'news' station, like, ten years ago. They're connected to folks at the highest levels of government. Like you said, Shiv, this is America, where if you are old, rich, and white enough, you can pretty much do anything you want."

"But people don't just show up missing, especially not college students, without some sort of massive manhunt. Did anybody tell anyone where we were going today?" Shiv asks.

I shake my head, remembering even before signing that NDA in the office, Chrissy and I were explicitly instructed in advance not to tell anyone what we were going to do.

"So, that's just it, then? We're all going to die down here, and there's nothing we can do about it? What's the point in even trying?"

"That doesn't make sense. If Krentler Media just wanted to kill a couple of college students—" I say.

"And one recent graduate..." PQ adds.

"Why go to all this trouble? Why cook up a fake story about an upcoming reality show, send us all the way out here, and create these puzzles? I think PQ is right. We are guinea pigs for a very real competition series that's going to happen. If that's true, it means there has to be a solution. They're playtesting this thing, right? They want to see what works and what doesn't. They want to see if it's possible to win."

"If they want us to win, why kill off a quarter of the team in the first ten minutes?" Shiv asks.

I shake my head, my heart heavy for Chrissy, knowing what I'm about to say will only make me feel worse. "As much as I hate to admit it, Chrissy wasn't a competitor. In fact, she didn't really do much at all. At school, they had a nickname for her."

"*Extra bookend*," PQ says, knowing her reputation as a slacker.

"I think the morgue was Krentler Media's attempt to literally light a fire under our asses to take this seriously. My guess is, the fact that they killed Chrissy so early will only help them long-term, as it shows them that proving this is all real early on will get us to play our hardest right from the jump."

"And they haven't even shown us any of the ghosts yet," Shiv says.

As if on cue, there is a distant sound of a woman wailing coming from somewhere outside our brick-basement room. Not just somewhere—everywhere. It seems to be emanating from the corners of the room, from the hallway in both directions. I can hear her above us and, I swear to God, somewhere below us as well. Shiv's eyebrows furrow, and her lips tighten, as if she has just been personally offended.

It's not the sound of Chrissy's crying, thank God. This voice sounds older, more somber, as if she has spent at least a century in constant mourning and has perfected her moans to the absolute pinnacle of bone-chilling despair.

"No, no, no, no," Shiv says. Without warning, she smacks herself on the side of her head with her palm.

"What is it?" PQ asks.

"It *can't* be her. There's just no way."

"Who?"

Shiv shakes her head. "It's been years. I was just a girl."

Across the room, the door sits slightly ajar. As I cross to look into the hallway, Shiv grabs me by the wrist.

"Don't go. *She's* out there."

"I'll only be a minute," I say, pulling my hand from Shiv's grip. "If this thing is a threat, we need to know *where* it is." The heavy metal door opens with a creak so loud I'm afraid it's going to catch the attention of the wailing woman.

I look down the hall to my left. Concrete walls and a labyrinth of pipes overhead confirm we're in the basement of The Propitius Hotel. My jaw drops when I turn to the right and see a woman in an ornamental black dress at the end of a long hall. Her head, covered in long white hair, is hung low, and she loudly laments, burying her covered face in a white handcloth massively stained by blood. There is a semi-transparency to her body, allowing me to see through her for a moment when she passes under one of the half-dozen lightbulbs hanging by a string across the ceiling. She's not walking so much as floating. I can't see her feet, but her movement is unnatural, no gait or bobbing to her efforts. Even though she's slowly approaching, I feel like she doesn't even notice me. My theory is proven correct when she makes a right turn into a room I can only guess is the morgue from which we just escaped.

"I'm going to follow her," I say.

"No, please," Shiv begs, softening into someone I haven't seen before. She's scared.

"Why? Do you know something I don't?" I ask, peering down the hall at the closed door through which the apparition passed.

"It sounded like the Bean Sidhe," she says.

*****

Investigate the sound. Turn to page 76.
Follow Shiv's advice. Turn to page 173.

Shiv starts to follow PQ into the guest room, but I grab her by the shoulder, risking her ire in response.

"How about you give him a minute? Let him get cleaned up and gather himself in private?" I say.

She frowns at my suggestion. "I think we should stick with him, just in case."

"He's just washing his hands. He'll be two seconds."

"A lot can happen in two seconds," Shiv says. "So far, we've had secret trapdoors, one of your own friends burned to death...We saw a mythical Banshee from my childhood, and we just had to solve a puzzle using human guts as the pieces. I'd say that's more than enough evidence to warrant some concern over any of us splitting up for any amount of time."

Shiv has a fair point. This hotel was built as a house of death long before a group of evil TV execs came in and made it *extra* dangerous.

I'm just beginning to regret my decision when the guest room door swings back open. PQ emerges, looking no worse for wear and using a towel to wring his hands dry. I let out a small sigh of relief.

"All right, I feel like a new man. Or at least, one that's not covered in death and chemicals. Where to next?"

Back in the hallway, there's a left turn ahead. Whatever is down that hall is projecting a rainbow of reds, greens, yellows, and blues against the drab wall.

"I think those lights are from the stained-glass windows in the lobby," I say. "We should probably head there to get our bearings and figure out what to do next."

My hunch is correct, and moments later, we step into the most well-lit room of our entire journey so far. On either side of the red double doors are intricately patterned stained glass windows, each with a large red circle in the center. I want to try the front doors, bang on them and scream for help, but I already know by now they're not going to let us go that easily.

"Hey, check this out," PQ says, inspecting the hotel's check-in desk.

There's a large black box with silver metal lining sitting on the table. Its lid is held on by hinges, and there's a simple button mechanism to open it, like on carry-on luggage. Plastered across the front in bold white lettering is: "Ectoplasmic Containment Unit." Before I have a chance to warn him, PQ presses the button, which sends the metal lock flying up on a spring. He lifts the lid, and I can see over his shoulder. The entire bottom and sides are lined in a shiny metallic sheeting.

"I think you're supposed to put the journal in there," PQ says, prompting me to move it from under my shoulder and into the box.

At this point, I have no idea what to expect. Nothing here seems simple enough to be taken at face value, so when I place the journal into the box, I do it carefully. I hold it out by two fingers, then drop the book into the box. As soon as it connects with the silver foil lining, the book erupts in crackles of purple lightning dancing around the box for a few seconds. The light show abruptly ends, and the book sits dormant, wisps of steam rising from it.

"I guess that's one down," I say.

"And two to go," a voice comes from above us.

My eyes trace along the staircase hugging the lobby wall, finding Lucy, our hostess and captor, leaning proudly against a rail. She's grinning down at us as casually as if we had just returned her dry cleaning.

I clench my fists, trying to bite back a sudden surge of anger. "You killed Chrissy!" I shout, wanting to run at her but knowing better.

Shiv apparently doesn't.

"You bitch!" she screams, then sprints toward the stairs.

Before she can reach the first step, the lights in the lobby flick out. Shiv skids to a halt when the lights come on and finds herself nearly face-to-face with a man in a brown tweed suit. He's standing on the stairs, holding onto an antique-looking rusty bone saw. His eyes are pure white, and yet somehow, I can feel them burning straight into my soul. He has round glasses, a bushy brown mustache, and a matching bowler hat straight from the nineteenth century. It's the ghost of Arthur Wilson—of that there is no doubt— and the only way to Lucy is through him.

At least Shiv knows better than to try and fight a ghost. She backs off, rejoining me and PQ in the center of the room.

Lucy mocks a look of shock on her face and raises her hand to her chest, as if she were clutching pearls. "Moi? I didn't kill anyone. If I recall from watching the footage, any one of you could have let her into your pods during that morgue fire. Let's not blame others for our own failures."

"What do you want from us?" Shiv growls. "What you're doing is sick!"

Lucy shakes her head. "I'm pretty sure I made it clear from the beginning that you would be beta testing a brand-new type of event. If you're unhappy with the game you signed up to play, you probably should have read the fine print more closely. That's also on you." Lucy sneers and nods her head.

"How many others have you done this to?" I ask.

"More than a few, less than a lot," Lucy says casually. "As I'm sure you can tell by now, there's a lot of moving pieces to this game, and before we can bring celebrities on to actually air this, we need to be prepared for a number of scenarios."

"I'm going to kill you before this day is done," Shiv says, her eyes narrowed to daggers.

"You're more than welcome to try," Lucy replies, "but I don't think you'll have much success getting through Wilson in his current state. You still need to find his spectacles and pocket watch before he's vulnerable, and threatening me isn't going to help you find them any easier. Of course, if you all behave yourselves, I can give you a clue to the next artifact."

I bite my tongue, like I'm sure Shiv and PQ are doing, knowing she has us over a barrel. She clearly holds all the cards, and unless we play along, finding a way out of this may very well be impossible.

After a few seconds of awkward silence, Lucy nods triumphantly. "That's better. So, are you all ready to hear the riddle? I'm only going to say it once." She clears her throat, and I try my best to focus. "In order for you to find the light, look for yourself in the dead of night. That's it. Best of luck!"

"Wait, that's the whole thing?" PQ asks.

Before Lucy can respond, the lights go out again, and by the time they're back on, both Lucy and the apparition of our famous serial killer have vanished.

"Crap. Anyone good at riddles?"

I shake my head. While I'm a great problem solver, it usually involves overcoming physical obstacles. Thinking outside the box only works for me when there's an actual box in front of me to work around. "Maybe it's got something to do with black lights? Those are both dark and light, I guess."

"And *where* have you seen a black light in this house so far?" Shiv asks with some extra attitude I really don't think is necessary. "I don't even think black lights were invented when this place was built."

My anger bubbles to the surface. The rage I just felt toward Lucy has to come out, and I find myself directing it at Shiv instead. "What, and Ectoplasmic Containment Units did? This place is rigged to high hell with modern traps. The only rule seems to be that there are no rules!"

"Whatever," she says, trying to dismiss me.

But I'm not done yet. "Seriously, Shiv, you think they had self-immolating morgues back in the day? How about weight-sensitive bowls where you have to drop in specific body parts? You think that was a popular game for the kids back then? I mean, crap, you think they had this place rigged up with cameras when it was built in nineteen oh-whatever?"

"That's enough, Jeremy. Christ."

"What, you don't like being spoken to like you're the asshole? Then maybe stop treating me that way and you'll find that it's easier if we work together."

Shiv looks like she wants to spit. "Yeah, and I'm just supposed to follow an arsehole who's scared of his own reflection, then, yeah? You couldn't even look at a hallway mirror without nearly crapping your pants."

"Hang on, I think you're onto something," PQ says.

"Damn right, I am. I say let *me* make the decisions for a while."

"Not that," PQ replies. "The riddle. In order for you to find the light, look for yourself in the dead of night. If I were planning to look at myself, I'd probably use a mirror, right?"

I nod. "Yeah, that makes sense to me. What about the rest?"

Shiv jumps in. "Also, how many mirrors would you say are in this hotel? We could spend all night just trying to find the right one."

PQ shakes his head. "I don't think so. We were meant to come out of the basement, right? That mirror in the hallway was almost impossible for us to miss. I feel like it has to be that one."

"Well, I've got another idea," Shiv says. "Instead of faffing about with some stupid riddle, how about we head upstairs and try to find out where Lucy just went off to? We know she's not a ghost. There has to be some sort of crew access nearby. If we can figure out where she went, maybe we can find a back way out of here."

*****

Search for a secret crew door upstairs. Turn to page 83.
Try and solve the riddle. Turn to page 21.

I don't think I'd be bragging if I were to say I have shouldered a significant portion of the responsibility in keeping our team moving forward in this house of death. But when it comes to dealing with potentially deadly spirits from Irish folklore randomly showing up in Southern California, I think it's a fair choice to defer to the local expert.

"Shiv, what do we do?" I ask, the sound of the wailing woman growing exponentially louder.

She looks at me, her eyes pure panic. Shiv's likely already going into shock from the blood loss. It doesn't help that we're now watching her own personal demon pass through a bookshelf as if there was nothing there.

"We have to run," Shiv says, as if it were the most obvious thing in the world. Even with her injured leg, Shiv makes an impressive dash for the library door.

By some small miracle, the Banshee passes into the room from the wall opposite the door. I don't waste any time looking a gift horse in the mouth and take off directly behind Shiv. She cuts a hard right out the door into the hall. The Banshee's weep turns into a shriek as I cross the threshold of the library. It's a sound so horrendous, so world-shatteringly loud, it physically blows me down from behind, as if I'd just been kicked by an entity made entirely of air. The glass sconces on the walls shatter, sending a hail of broken glass around us.

"We have to keep moving." Shiv tugs at my shoulder. Her voice is so light and tinny, it barely cuts through the ringing in my pounding head. She's somehow already back on her feet.

Blood is running from her ears, and the warmth trickling down my jaw and onto my neck makes me suspect I'm suffering from the same condition. I let her pull me up, and we scramble down the hall.

I don't look back.

We make a right, then another. I'm the one pulling Shiv along now. Her leg has started to drag her down. We haven't heard the Banshee since her initial scream, but it doesn't make me ease up. Even though she moves without her feet ever touching the ground, I can *feel* her nearby.

I'm about halfway down the hall when claws scrape across my back, coming from the right. Shiv screams and is yanked away from my grasp.

The Banshee has her. She must have come soaring through the wall at the spirit equivalent of a full sprint, gripping Shiv with hands ending in blackened claws. While the Banshee continues its flight through the opposite wall, Shiv slams into it, her head and shoulder leaving an indent. Shiv falls to the ground like a ragdoll, crumpling in a tangle of arms and legs.

I know I should get up and run. Shiv's dead—I can tell just from the impossible positioning of her neck. But I can't help myself. I'm not ready to be in here all alone.

"Shiv," I call out, kneeling at her side and feeling for a pulse. My suspicion is confirmed when I feel a knot of something hard, a piece of bone crammed into a space it clearly shouldn't be.

I look up at the wall in front of us, doing my best to accept my fate. It still does little to prepare me for the grotesque face of fury that comes soaring at me, her eyes a bright red, her mouth a gaping hole into an abyss of absolute nothingness.

Her already blood-soaked claws pierce both my shoulders, sending me to the ground. I want to bring my hands up to defend myself, but she's severed whatever tendons I need to make my arms do anything at all. Instead, I'm forced to watch helplessly as she carves away my chest and stomach, wondering what organs are flying around me in red meaty chunks.

*****

Try again. Turn to page 132.

*****

I make a hard right and run down the hallway, past a corridor and a room with an open door. Either sweat or blood runs from my forehead and drips into my eye, and in the moment it takes for me to blink it out, Arthur Wilson appears mere feet in front of me, his scalpel aimed at my face. I skid to a stop, my ankle nearly buckling, and I push through the pain, taking off in the other direction and ducking into the open door on my right.

Unlike the rest of this gloomy hotel, this room has bright powder-blue wallpaper. Inside is a baby's crib, a box full of toys, and a toddler's rocking horse. The nursery.

What I don't see anywhere is a way out of here. The light overhead flickers, but this time, Arthur doesn't teleport. No need, as he has me cornered.

Arthur steps into the doorway, leaning against the frame and grinning at me. His scalpel is small but lethal in his hands.

I made a mistake coming into this tiny room. My only option is to fight. I grab the rocking horse and hold it like a shield.

Arthur cocks his head back and silently laughs. With almost no effort, he grabs onto the rocking horse and yanks it away from me. I scramble to the side when he steps toward me, bumping into the crib on the far wall opposite the door. Then I maneuver into the corner of the room.

I can't die like this, cowering in a corner while an evil ghost carves me up—a practice run for some seriously screwed-up reality show. Crouching, I grab two of the legs on the wooden crib to put something between me and Wilson, but it doesn't budge. The legs are bolted to the floor, but holy shit...Underneath the crib is a small hidden door, just big enough for me to crawl through on my stomach.

Arthur is taking his time but within arm's reach. The merciless grin on his face makes me believe he has no idea

I've seen the hidden door. I need to time this perfectly and hope the hidden door is unlocked.

Arthur raises the scalpel over his head, blade supported by his outstretched pointer finger for maximum control. I'm watching for the blade, but mostly, I'm concentrating on his eyes. Even though the eyeballs are completely white, his lids and eyebrows convey a world of emotion. Elation, concentration, but mostly hunger. It's the bloodlust that gives away the moment he intends to strike.

Before his arm is even moving, I'm hurling my body at the trapdoor under the crib like a baseball player sliding into home plate. My hands connect with the small panel and push it open. My fingers find an edge and pull me into the room. Wilson's scalpel thuds into the floorboards behind me.

This room is cramped, its walls just exposed framing with dozens of wires running along every surface. There's a series of flatscreen panels, several narrow paths following spaces in between the hotel's walls, and a black metal ladder leading both up and down.

It takes a second to recognize the skinny guy with mussed brown hair sitting in front of a laptop. He's the dude from the front desk when I first entered Krentler Media. I think his name is Todd.

Despite my terror and exhaustion, I'm still chock-full of adrenaline. This motherfucker has been watching us this whole time.

His eyes are wide with fear when he stammers out, "Um, you're not supposed to be in here."

I slam him into the wall with my forearm and press my other against his throat. It's a trick I learned from Shiv.

"You did this to us," I growl.

"Not me personally," he says. "It's a collaborative effort, and I'm just one small piece of a—"

I push so hard it shuts him up. "You watched us get tortured and killed and did nothing to stop it!"

For the moment, all the fear has drained out of me. I don't know where Wilson is, don't care. All that matters is me and Todd.

*****

Kill Todd. Turn to page 150.
Spare Todd. Turn to page 175.

"How about you give that hand a rest and let me take the next one." Shiv carefully eyes *The Ripper* sitting in the middle of a minefield, where every inch is potentially deadly. "I just need to find something to give me an edge…"

I look at the pair of extra books on the floor, which fell off the table during my last disastrous run. "What if you used these? You could, like, throw them at the book on the table and try to knock it off."

Shiv twists her face up like she's sucking on a lime. "I like the idea of the extra books. I *hate* the idea of throwing them. What if there was another way to use them? As some sort of armor? We've seen the shards can't pierce through a cover. How about I just stuff my vest full of books, to at least protect all my vital bits?"

I feel so stupid for suggesting tossing books around when her alternative is obviously better. She's able to easily wedge one book between the collar of her vest and her head to protect her neck, but once we slide the other book to cover her mid-back, we realize there's a lot more room for books. I look around the room and grin.

"If only there was somewhere that we could find a few more books to stuff into your vest. Nobody's going to miss a few of these, are they?" I ask, venturing to one of the library's walls and pulling a few from the shelf.

For once, Shiv and I are on exactly the same page, and I swear she comes damn close to actually giving me a smile.

"All right, I think I'm fully stacked," Shiv says once we have her entire vest so crammed with books, she almost looks like a turtle.

"Keep your arms tucked under your chest when you jump," I say. "That way, you keep your armor as the most obvious target. Only reach out when you've got a clear shot at grabbing the book."

I expect an irritated response, but instead, she just nods at me.

"Okay. Here goes nothing." Shiv backs almost to the far wall of the room, giving herself plenty of space for a running start. She uses all of it, leaping high and tucking her arms into her chest in her best impression of a torpedo. Shiv lands on the table with a loud *thunk*, and she lets out a surprised *oof*, as if the air's been knocked out of her.

The first shard falls from overhead. It's one of the largest in the chandelier, nearly a foot long. It would have easily pierced through her neck if it weren't for the thick hardback propped in that exact position. Unfortunately, the weight of the shard embedded in the book causes it to slide sideways and fall onto the table, removing her shielding. Realizing this, Shiv army crawls a foot or so forward until she is within reaching distance of the book.

Three more shards drop, almost simultaneously. One *thunks* into a book in the back of her vest. Another misses her, landing just to her right. The third is a direct hit, landing on the upper part of her right thigh. It slices through skin and muscle with a soft *slink*, followed by a gasp from Shiv.

She doesn't let that stop her. Her hand shoots forward, snatching the book and holding it over her neck, replacing the one previously protecting that area. The only problem is, with her arms tucked into her chest, she can't back up fast enough.

More shards fall. A book protects one, but another seems to sink just out of range of her defenses, right into her shoulder.

The chandelier drops an oversized dagger that lands in the exact place where her fingers are gripping the book. Shiv screams as three little fleshy sausages roll onto the table.

She's not going to make it. I rush over, grab her ankles, and yank her off the table with all my might. I'm only slightly ashamed to admit my first thought is to make sure Shiv pulled the copy of *The Ripper* off the table with her. The book is sitting next to us, though its cover is soaked in blood.

Shiv holds up her hand, and instead of pain or fear, there's nothing but rage. She stares at the stumps of her pointer, middle, and ring finger, all severed below the first knuckle and pumping out spurts of blood, like a trio of squirt guns. I offer to find something to make into a tourniquet, but she scowls and shoves her hand under her armpit, pressing as hard as she can until a dark stain spreads.

"Pull the crap out of my back first," she says, panting.

I circle around, and on the count of three, I pull a shard from her shoulder and another from her thigh. If it were me in this situation, I would probably be crying like a baby by now, but instead, all I see before me is a red-faced woman who looks like she's on the verge of murder.

"Is there anything else I can do?" I ask.

"Yeah, put that last damn book in the slot, and let's get the hell out of here."

I do as she says, after prying the huge shard out of the bloodstained cover. Once all the books are on their special little shelf, I take a step back, waiting for the spectacles to appear via some mechanical function or ingenious contraption.

Without warning, the entire chandelier drops from the ceiling, exploding against the table and sending thousands of crystal shards flying, shrapnel in all directions.

Shiv has her back pressed against the table and is, thankfully, insulated from the majority of the impact. PQ and I, on the other hand, aren't so lucky. I lift my arms to cover my face, but the glass splinters are too fast and too sharp, slicing across my cheek and chin. A tiny spike pierces my ear and remains lodged in the cartilage. Several dozen little pieces rip through my hoodie and pants, leaving stinging stains of red all over.

When all is said and done, I have what probably amounts to two dozen tiny new wounds, though as far as I can tell, none seem serious.

"Shiv, PQ, you guys make it through that all right?"

From under the table, Shiv gripes, "I don't know that I would say I'm all right, but I'm no worse for wear than I was a few seconds ago. What about you, PQ?"

The fact he hasn't answered either of us makes my forehead hot with panic. I can't see him through the wreckage of the chandelier on the table, but as I move around to get a better view of him on the couch, I realize why he's having trouble responding. A shard seems to have sliced through the side of his neck. He's holding his hand up to his throat, blood oozing between his fingers. PQ opens and closes his mouth, trying his hardest to produce any sort of sound, but there's only a rasping breath being drowned out by his blood.

I want to run to him, to find some way to help. Instead, I just stand there, like a total goon, completely frozen by the knowledge that I'm watching yet another person in my life die before my eyes and there's nothing I can do about it.

It doesn't take long. After a few more seconds of what looks like the most desperate attempt at communication I've ever seen, PQ's hand drops from his neck, and his eyes drift away from me, staring out vacantly into nothingness.

"Christ," Shiv says when she finally gets to her feet.

"He didn't deserve that."

"I know this is going to make me sound like a real arsehole, but do you think, maybe, this is for the best? Like, get it all over with quick, instead of having to suffer through all those spider bites slowly eating away at him?"

I hate the fact that this morning, when I woke up, the hardest decision in my life was between Honey Nut Cheerios and Frosted Flakes, and now I'm weighing the pros and cons of a fast death versus a slow and agonizing one. At this point, I hold no delusion that Shiv and I are going to leave this hotel alive, but for just a few moments, I let my mind wonder what a life after today could even look like. No matter what happens, I can feel deep in my core, nothing in my life is ever going to be the same again.

I'm brought out of my head by a new sound, one that just keeps making things worse. Whoever at Krentler Media is watching us right now really loves to kick us when we're down.

From somewhere outside the library, a woman is wailing, and immediately, I know who it is.

The Banshee.

*****

Fight. Turn to page 3.
Cry. Turn to page 105.
Ask Shiv. Turn to page 122.

I run through the door labeled "Cigar Room," hoping to find some sort of hidden passage or something to possibly get me back to the first floor. It's a long shot, but my panicked brain can't think of a better idea.

The room is small, without much to search beyond some cigar boxes, a decanter of liquor, some books on a shelf, and a fireplace with a suspiciously fake-looking log display. When I grab one of the logs, the entire fireplace grate comes out with it, revealing a drop in the chimney leading to some room on the first floor. This is just what I need to circle around to meet Shiv back in the lobby.

Black soot puffs around me when I slam my back into the brick wall of the chimney. I'm getting ready to prop myself against the other side of the brick chute, but as I crouch, the door to the cigar room swings open.

Arthur Wilson stands in its frame, showing me his blade as if it were some sort of promise. He moves toward me in bizarre, disjointed steps, brandishing the scalpel in front of his face. I climb into the chimney, tuck my head into my armpit to avoid choking on the ash, and slide down into darkness until my legs press against nothing but air and my butt collides with the phony fireplace logs of the first floor.

Only, I don't stop there.

The force of my fall knocks the second fireplace out, and I'm descending again to the basement. I'm somehow lucky enough to catch my feet against the wall, slowing my fall, but my whole body aches. It's not just the pain of my back scraping against brick, or my rear colliding with the fireplace. It's like there are a thousand little pinpricks happening all over my body. I don't get a good look at what it is until I free fall from the bottom of the chute, nearly five feet into a pile of sand and ash cushioning my landing. When I see what's causing all the pinpricks, I almost wish I'd just died in the chimney, unaware.

I'm covered in spiders—brown recluses, like the ones that crawled all over me in the opium den, like the one single bite on my ankle which has caused me near agony from the moment it happened.

Now, hundreds of them are delivering their caustic venom into my skin, my veins. I try to swipe them off, scramble away and up to my feet. My back presses against something that makes the spider bites pale in comparison to the burning pain.

Throwing myself forward, I slam my chest against the ground, hopefully crushing some of the spiders. I manage to turn around and look at the thing that burned me. It's a furnace with a gate, like teeth, housing a raging fire. A surge of pain grips me, and my lips curl into an involuntary snarl. My eyes squeeze shut.

When I open them, Arthur Wilson is standing directly in front of me, next to the furnace. I search for an exit from this room, but there's no way I'd be able to make it without being caught by Arthur first.

I wait for him to make his move, to slit my throat with his precision blade. Instead, he reaches to his side, grips the handle of the furnace door, then pulls it open, all without ever looking away from me.

Movement stirs beyond the normal destructive dance of fire. A hand bursts forth from inside, its skin sending licks of flames from it as if it were the very source of the fire. The melted, barely recognizable body of my brother, Brian, crawls out of the furnace, leaving darkness behind.

Another wave of pain from the spider bites forces my whole body to contract, but I'm able to keep my eyes open. My burning brother staggers toward me and falls to his knees. The heat radiating off him is so intense, my eyebrows singe. He reaches his arms out as if to give me a hug.

The last thing I see as my body catches fire is Wilson. His mask is pulled down, revealing a huge grin filled with yellow mangled teeth.

*****

Try again. Turn to page 172.

I run straight, through an archway immediately leading to a series of twists and turns. The lights flicker constantly, and suddenly, Arthur Wilson is everywhere. In one second, his face is mere inches from mine, mask off and licking the tip of his scalpel until black blood pours down his chin. A moment later, he's behind me, swiping at my calf with his blade, then my arm, my rib. It's death by a thousand cuts. He moves so quickly, there's nothing I can do but run and try to protect my face, my forearms getting sliced to ribbons.

I enter a long hallway with giant paintings of Arthur Wilson along with an older man in a blue suit, who I can only assume to be his father. The lights stay on, and the specter previously delivering a flurry of shallow cuts is gone. Instead, I'm confronted with the looming figures of history. The only face more severe than Arthur's in these gloomy portraits is his father's, whose eyes show a coldness even Arthur can't manage.

I near the single door at the end of the hall. Its knob turns, and the door opens with an ominous creak. The room is painted in color and built into an octagonal-shaped side turret completely covered in intricate patterns of stained glass. The setting sun sends reds, blues, yellows, and greens in all directions in what seems like a large bedroom. The color is so overwhelming, it takes me a minute to notice the pair of rotting skeletons sitting in chairs up against one of the windows. One is in a dress, while the other wears a blue suit identical to the paintings in the hallway.

On a desk against the wall sits a Bunsen burner cooking something in a large black pot. Beyond it, at the far end of the room, is a door. When I'm two steps into the room, the shadow of the hallway lights behind me flicker. I turn around, searching for Arthur Wilson to appear in the doorway, but instead, I see nothing.

Actually, it's *more* than nothing.

Something's missing.

I turn to run for the door and am greeted by Arthur Wilson holding the black pot, which has just gone missing from his desk. Before I have time to react, he's throwing a steaming black liquid in my face. It burns unlike anything I've ever experienced before. I try to wipe it away with my hands, but my fingers get stuck to what feels like a vat of hot glue.

I can't even pull my hands away from my cheeks. It's like they're instantly seared into place. I'm falling, and my head hits the ground hard.

The only relief I get from the burning tar is when the cold metal of a scalpel presses against my throat.

*****

Try again. Turn to page 172.

Not only is Arthur now in human form, but I'm the one with the weapon. I raise the bone saw over my shoulder and lunge forward, swinging for his throat. Arthur raises a hand, deflecting the blow from my intended target, but I hack off several of his fingers in the process. His hollow eyes go wide in shock when his digits fall to the ground, turning into a clear goo as they hit the floor.

I never believed I could be capable of murder, but this isn't a man. This is a monster, and I hope he can feel the pain, the same as when it happened to Shiv. I want to make him feel every ounce of agony he's put us through.

But there's no time for that. I need to finish this.

I come at him again with the saw, this time pushing it forward with my other hand supporting the blade, driving it toward his throat. He retreats, jumping backward until he's pressed against the wall.

I'm pushing forward fast and hard enough to close the gap. The blade connects with his throat, the serrated teeth puncturing his pale flesh. I rip the saw to the left, feeling the rusted metal teeth grind and tear at his skin and muscle. Black sludge oozes from his throat, changing colors when it falls into a clear sludge, then quickly absorbs into the floor.

There's no stopping now. I press even harder, dragging the blade back and forth, staring Arthur in the eyes. The blade chews through his tendons, throat, and spine.

Arthur's head topples to the ground and melts into the floor. His body quickly follows, leaving clear wet streaks, pouring itself out like spoiled milk. In the end, all that's left is a golden amulet with a red gem in the center.

It takes all I have to bend over and grab the amulet. I expect it to feel like it's coated in Jell-o, but it's only slightly sticky, like hand sanitizer evaporating into nothing. I'm also shocked to discover the amulet is made entirely of plastic. In fact, the gem isn't even a real gem at all. It's just one big hollow replica, like something I would find at Party City.

This can't possibly be the actual Amulet of Duriel. But then I have to remind myself, there is no such thing as a real Amulet of Duriel. However Krentler Media was able to summon real ghosts into this house is beyond me, but it has nothing to do with this cheap toy.

Nevertheless, the last part of my job is to destroy the amulet, so that's what I intend to do. I walk over to the second-floor balcony and stand next to Shiv's body. Her hand hangs just over the edge, and I wish there was some way I could thank her for saving my life.

"All right, Shiv, here goes nothing." I throw the amulet at the wood floor as hard as I can.

A blinding red light explodes from the amulet, and a strong gust of wind sends the nearby chandelier swinging. Even though it holds, the sound of hundreds of little crystals jingling against each other makes me thankful I'm up here, not down on the lobby floor, where the amulet has shattered into about a dozen plastic shards. But there's more to it than that. Another layer.

There always is.

There's a glimmer of metal peeking out from one of the larger pieces of the amulet. While the amulet itself was hollow, there was something inside. It looks like a key.

In the last—I don't even know how many—hours, my definition of *hurry* has changed dramatically, but it's what I do to get down the stairs and retrieve the key, spending as little time under the swaying chandelier as possible. Once I'm clear of the chandelier's splash zone, I inspect the key a little closer. It's made of tarnished brass, with faded red and white candy cane stripes going down the shaft.

A confusing mix of hope and frustration pass over me. For a second, I was really hoping it would simply be a key to the front door and I could just get the hell out of here.

Instead, I get another clue to this never-ending puzzle house. At this point, I'm fully dragging my foot, making my way to the barber shop. Thankfully, it's not far from the lobby, and I don't have to climb those damn stairs again.

The key turns easily in the hole, and I find myself in a small but otherwise normal-seeming old-fashioned barber shop. There are two chairs sitting on rusted metal poles, with a reclining handle on the side. I don't have the energy to solve any more puzzles, so I collapse into one of the chairs.

Theoretically, Arthur Wilson is gone, and the Amulet of Duriel is destroyed, so unless a crew member appears with a shotgun in the next five minutes, I think I've earned a little rest. I pull the crank to see if the chair eases back, and my heart flies into my throat when the floor opens and swallows me and the chair whole.

I'm soaring downward, holding onto the arms of the chair to keep from hitting the carved stone walls surrounding me. The temperature drops, and the world grows dark, then just as quickly returns me to the dim world of orange lights. My descent slows, and my chair ends its journey in some sort of a mine shaft deep underground.

It's not so much a mine shaft as there have been walls erected on either side of the tunnel to make it seem almost like an office. There's a table in front of me with two metal chairs. One of them is filled by my captor, Lucy; the other is empty. Standing by one of the doors is a woman who appears to be around the same age as Lucy, with black hair and firetruck-red lipstick. She stands at attention with a pistol holstered at her hip.

"Congratulations!" Lucy exclaims, reaching down to the floor beside her and pulling up two glasses and an uncorked bottle of champagne. "You're today's big winner." She pours a glass for herself and another that she sets on the opposite side of the table. "And to think, Charlotte over here was ready to bet me twenty dollars we would have four bodies on our hands."

I'm confused, angry, and in an extreme amount of pain. Sharing champagne with the person who just tricked me into muddling around a haunted murder mansion for the day is the last thing I was expecting to happen. She clearly catches on to my skepticism to join her, probably because I'm still in the barber chair.

Lucy gestures a hand to the seat across from her. "I promise, no more games. You won the playtest. Not just that, we have some very potentially exciting offers for you, if you'll come join me and answer some questions about how to make the experience better in the future."

*****

Refuse Lucy's offer. Turn to page 148.
Take a seat. Turn to page 179.

It could take hours to read the title of every book on the library walls. I somehow doubt that's what this show's producers want their audience to watch, so I direct my attention to the manageable stack of books on the table. Unsure of what else to do, I pick one up and quickly shake it, spine-side up, hoping for something out of place to fall from between the pages. No such luck.

"So that's your plan, then? Give the books a good shake and see what comes out?" Shiv asks.

"Unless you have a better plan." I let a twinge of irritation come through. So far, Shiv's been consistently critical of my plans, only for me to have led us through this whole process. At this point, I wonder if there's anything I could possibly do to get her to trust my judgment.

I reach for a second book to shake out, while Shiv decides to ignore my suggestion completely and instead focuses on the blank piece of paper and ink pot on the far corner of the table. After a few seconds, she gives me something between a laugh and a harumph.

"All right, smart guy. I don't want to distract you from your very important job over there, but what do you make of this?" She's holding the piece of paper up to the chandelier hanging overhead, and if I squint, I can make out depression marks on the page, as if someone had written a message on the piece of paper just on top of this and left behind a ghost of their words.

While I'm redirecting my attention to Shiv's paper, I'm distracted by something sharp suddenly slicing into my forearm. I drop the book when my hand recoils on reflex, and I see a reflective piece of small etched glass with a sharpened tip stabbed into the table.

"What the hell was that?" I clutch at my forearm, feeling a warm wetness spreading through the torn sleeve of my hoodie.

The chandelier sways slightly, hanging directly over the table. The ornamental lighting piece is covered in dozens, if not hundreds of similar crystal spikes of varying sizes dangling from every inch. I shut my eyes and let out a heavy breath, realizing, once again, we're about to endure something incredibly unpleasant.

"Get back," I tell Shiv, taking a few steps away from the table to give myself some space from the weaponized chandelier.

It's only with that distance that I notice an empty space on the side of the table. It's a single bookshelf long enough to hold around four books.

"I think I figured it out," I say. "There's a little bookshelf in the table to slot in certain books. I bet if we can figure out what books to put in there, it'll give us the spectacles. Problem is, that chandelier is going to drop decorative knives on us every time we reach out to grab a book."

Shiv opens her mouth, then closes it and squints at the scene before us, her hands resting on her hips. "Hang on. What if we just move the table?" She makes sure to stay out of the chandelier's radius and grabs the table by the legs.

I don't have a ton of hope in her plan, though I keep my mouth shut and watch her struggle to get the table to move.

"Looks like the bugger's bolted to the floor." Shiv shakes out her arms. "We're just going to have to be quick about it."

Luckily, during her initial retreat, she managed to hold onto the paper with the faded writing and now gets a good look at it.

"It's definitely a list of books. If you hold it up to the light just right, you can see some of the names."

She walks over to PQ, who is inspecting his wounds. They no longer just look like little swollen bites. His arm is polka-dotted in red spots of exposed tissue underneath skin slowly being eaten away by venom.

"Hey, you feeling up to being our caller for this? You name the books, and we'll track'em down?"

He doesn't seem to notice her. PQ gently pokes at one of the dozens of glistening sores, then reels back with a sharp hiss.

"Hey, I'm talking to you," Shiv repeats, this time grabbing him by the hand and pulling it away from his blistering arm. "You need to focus on something other than the bites, and I have a mission for you. We need you in the game now, yeah?"

It's as if PQ is operating on a slight delay. He waits a second, staring into the distance, before snapping to attention and accepting the paper from her. "Yeah, sorry. I'm on it. What do you need me to do again?"

"Find the names of books on that list, read'em out, then we'll snatch them and put them in their hidey hole." Shiv gives PQ more patience than she's ever given me.

PQ nods and holds the paper up to the chandelier, angling it around slightly until he can make out the faint depressions on it.

"Okay, the first one is *A History of Amputations*, by...something Williamson."

Shiv and I stalk around the table, looking at all the books with exposed titles facing outward. Because of the nature of the pile, there are about a half-dozen books completely obscured inside the stack at the center. It would require one of us to lean our whole upper torso across the table to reach those books, and even then, it would take some time to clear them all away.

"Found it," Shiv says, pointing to a book thankfully nowhere near the stack. It seems like a fairly easy grab, sitting with a few others near one of the edges. Once again, Shiv limbers herself, bouncing around to psych herself up.

"Be careful," I say.

"I got it, I got it." She waves me off. After several feints, she darts in and reaches for the book.

She's quick, but not quick enough.

As she's pulling back, an arrow-shaped crystal embeds itself in her arm, just above the wrist. Shiv drops the book to the floor and spins around, swearing a string of curses and reaching for, then pulling her hand away from, the shard sticking out of her arm.

"Are you okay?" I ask, taking a step toward her but keeping enough distance so I don't crowd her space.

"Christ, I think it's in the bone." She touches the crystal ever so slightly with her index finger and immediately looks like she regrets it. Shiv turns to me, her eyes plain with fear. "I just gotta pull it out quick, right? Just get it over with?"

I feel like she's not actually asking, but more seeking validation for her thoughts. In movies when people are shot with arrows or impaled by rebar pipes, they always say not to take it out. In real life, I have no idea. It's such a small wound, though, I can't imagine removing it will make her injury any worse.

"You want me to pull it out? I could do it really fast."

She considers me for a second, then shakes her head. "No. I'll do it." Shiv takes several deep breaths, reaches up, and yanks the shard out of her arm. It seems like it requires more force than she expects, and I can almost hear a pop when it flings free.

I don't for a second think Shiv was exaggerating about it being embedded in the bone.

While she holds a hand over her wrist, I find the book on the ground and slot it into the end of the shelf. It fits snugly, with not even an inch to spare on the top. I hope this is a good sign we are on the right track.

"I'll take the next one," I say. "PQ, you got another for us?"

"Yeah, I think I can make this one out. It's just called *Human Physiology*, but the guy's got a silly name. Robley Dunglison, M.D."

"Wait, I remember seeing that name." I round the table to a small stack of books about four high. The one I need is brown, and the title is partially faded, but the author's name is as clear as day, written about three times larger. "This has to be it. I got this one."

Having seen twice already how fast the chandelier is at dropping knives, I come up with an idea. Since the book is at the top of a stack, I press my fingers together to make my hand as flat and narrow a target as possible. I then swipe it across the table, as if I were using my arm as a baseball bat. The book goes flying, and just behind my hand, an eight-inch shard of crystal comes stabbing down into the stack.

"Look at you, getting all fancy." Shiv retrieves the book and slots it into the shelf.

With two in, I feel like my initial estimate was right on, with us needing a total of four books. "What else ya got, PQ?" I ask.

"Oh, no way," he says, nearly chuckling but stopping himself short. "I know this one from TV. *Gray's Anatomy: Descriptive and Surgical*, by Henry Gray."

"Would you imagine the luck?" I spot the book immediately—sitting one lower in the same pile where I found the last one. "Let's try this again."

I swing my arm even more vigorously this time, with the intention of knocking several books off the table at once, but a huge shard, at least a foot long, falls from the chandelier, landing between my hand and the books. My palm slams into the razor's edge at full speed, slicing deep into the tendons. I scream in pain. Blood gushes from the wound, and I squeeze my hand shut as hard as I can to staunch the bleeding.

"Those sons of bitches," Shiv grumbles. She grabs the chandelier shard that previously stabbed her and uses it to cut a line out of her sleeve. "Here, the cut looks deep. You're gonna want to tie it off." She hands me the strip of fabric.

I do as she says, and Shiv crouches on the floor to retrieve some books. Apparently, all that force was good for something, aside from lacerating my hand. I managed to knock three books off the table, one being *Gray's Anatomy*.

"At least we got three down. Just one to go," I say. "Give me some good news, PQ. you figure out the last one?"

"Sort of. I've got good news and bad news. It looks like whoever wrote this one wrote something else over the title. There's no way for me to make it out. All I got is the author. F. Gerstatt. I hope that's enough."

Shiv and I spend a solid five minutes studying the rest of the books on the table. We find one called *The Ripper*, by F. Gerstatt, within the first minute or so but spend the rest of the time making sure there aren't any other books by that author.

Shiv shakes her head. "Well, I've got a good news, bad news situation for you. The good news is there's only one book, but the bad news is it's smack dab in the middle of this table."

She's not wrong. The book is directly under the most central—and largest—shard on the entire chandelier.

"So, who's turn is it, then?" she asks me, never taking her eyes off the book.

*****

It's my turn. Turn to page 18.
Let Shiv decide. Turn to page 128.

"You're joking, right?" I ask. "After what you just did to me and my friends, you seriously expect me to sit down and give you feedback on how to make this place more fucked up? You gotta be out of your mind." I gesture to the armed woman in the corner of the room. "If you didn't have a gun-toting guard on hand, I'd be tempted to try and stop you from ever doing this again."

Lucy lets out a heavy sigh and shakes her head. I legitimately can't tell if it's genuine or performative.

"If that's your stance, we at Krentler Media will respect your decision. Besides, we have more than enough footage to analyze without your commentary." Lucy snaps her fingers, and the guard joins her. "This is Charlotte. She will escort you off the premises and drive you back home. I shouldn't have to say this, but just so we're absolutely crystal clear, I will anyways. You signed an NDA before entering here, with a lifetime guarantee not to speak a single word about what transpired today to a single person. I hope you realize by now that we take that NDA very seriously. Should you do anything to jeopardize our mission, we will have to take extreme measures to silence you. Is that clear?"

I nod, but I'm still waiting for the other shoe to drop. There's no way she's going to let me out of here, just like that. Right? I mean, Krentler Media is a mega conglomerate, but they're not immune to the law, are they?

At first, I had sworn to myself that if I ever got out, I would shout from the rooftops in order to get justice for Chrissy, PQ, and Shiv. Now, I don't know. Is this a secret I can keep for my whole life?

Charlotte takes me through a door and leads me down a series of winding tunnels. I think about my former teammates' parents, imagine them calling to check-in, the panic when their children never answer, the grief when they're declared missing. And even worse, being forced to spend the rest of their lives wondering if their children are dead or simply vanished. I don't think I could live with myself, knowing what I know and not being able to give them closure.

The tunnels end abruptly in a room that simply has a pit in it and an overwhelming smell of decay that makes me gag. It doesn't take a genius to know what's down there.

"So, this is what happens to all the 'winners?'" I ask Charlotte, turning to face her.

Her gun is already pointed at my head.

I guess that answers *that* question.

*****

The correct answer was to take a seat. Turn to page 179.

I push harder against his trachea, pouring every ounce of strength I have left into making Todd pay for what they've done to me. His arms flap and smack against my body, but his attempts to stop me are feeble.

Todd drives a bony knee into my stomach. It's not enough to fully knock the wind out of me, but I stagger back and completely lose my grip on him. I'm expecting him to follow up with a fist to the head, a radio call for backup, or for the little pissant to just high-tail it out of there. Instead, he gapes at me, frozen in terror. Somehow, his complete lack of self-preservation skills only serves to send me into even more of a rage.

He stammers out a few words, begging for his life, before my anger sends me completely out of my mind. I grab his face with my large, uninjured palm and slam it as hard as I can into the wall behind him. The sound of his skull crunching against the wooden beams turns my stomach. It instantly drains me of my bloodlust, replacing it with an overwhelming crash of regret.

His body goes slack, and the panic in his eyes melts into a blank stare, reminding me of the faces of Brian and Chrissy back in the library. I let go of his head, and his dead body falls to the floor.

What have I done? My throat tightens, my chest feels like it's being squeezed by a noose, and I take a step back, watching Todd's lifeless body fall to the floor.

I did this. All on my own. I just wanted to escape, not to hurt anyone. Not to kill. Even when Lucy was taunting us, I never realistically expected I would be capable of taking her life. Yet here I stand, shaking over the body of some PA who just happened to be there when I came through.

I am a killer.

What's done is done, and Arthur's still out there. On one of the TV screens, Shiv's trapped in the hallway leading toward the stairs. Arthur has abandoned the scalpel and instead is wielding a large axe, stalking toward her. If I don't stop him, he's going to kill her.

I am a killer.

I slip back into the nursery and run toward Shiv's position. When I get there, she is writhing on the floor, clutching her injured hand while staring up at Wilson. I can only see him from behind, but he's got the axe leveraged over his head, gripping it by the base with both hands. I charge at him, tucking low to tackle, but I fly right through him and land on top of Shiv. Recovering fast enough to push myself up, I give her a chance to wriggle free.

She looks between me and the axe-wielding maniac ghost behind.

"It's okay," I say, knowing what's about to happen. Get to the box. Save yourself."

Shiv scrambles out from beneath me just as the axe buries into my spine. My legs collapse, and while my back is sending unbearable arcs of pain throughout my torso, my legs go completely numb. My body is lifted from the floor when Arthur tries to pull his axe out of me. Eventually, my body weight is enough to free it from the embedded blade, and I drop to the floor with a *thump.*

My body is made of nothing but pain—no feeling or control of anything below my belly button. But I have one last job to do. With what little strength I have left in my arms, I turn myself over to face my attacker.

I can't see Shiv anywhere, so I assume she made it. Now it's just me and Arthur. He raises his axe again, ready for the final blow, when a purple crackle of lightning suddenly dances across him and he sneers in pain.

If I had working legs, this would be the perfect time to escape or come up with a new plan, or do something. Anything. Instead, I just watch him recover enough to raise the axe. Before it comes down onto my head, a tremendous sense of peace washes over me. This is the right way to go.

I am a killer.

*****

The correct answer was to spare Todd. Turn to page 175.

I shake my head, and it's the hardest thing I've ever had to do. The real Brian wouldn't want me to spend an eternity in agony just so I could be with him. He would want me to live my life and keep fighting to survive, no matter what.

"I'm sorry," I say to my poor little brother.

He wails at me to wait, but I can't. I circle around him and make my way back into the hotel's halls.

When I shut the museum door behind me, his desperate cries silence, as if I flicked off a light switch. My legs tremble, and I lean against the wall just to stay standing. Whatever energy I had left, most likely pure adrenaline, is gone. My ankle hurts. The cut across my hand throbs. I'm overcome with a strong desire to just sit down here and rest a minute.

Shiv screams. It's distant, but she's still upstairs somewhere. At the end of the hall, my reflection appears in the tall mirror, which turned out to be a secret door. That means I'm not too far from the lobby.

It takes an incredible amount of effort to force myself back into action. I limp toward my only other surviving companion, each footfall a reminder the wound in my ankle is spreading. Even though there's nothing to be gained, I'm now constantly fighting an urge to lift my pant leg and see how much of my skin the spider's acidic venom has eaten through.

I push it out of my mind and make a hard left into the lobby. Shiv is on the upper balcony, standing opposite Wilson, who is blocking her from reaching the stairs. In her hand is the broken-off leg of a wooden chair. It comes to a splintered spike that looks deadly, in any other situation. Arthur is holding a rusted bone saw, completely still and waiting for Shiv to make the first move.

"Shiv!" I call out, far enough back I have a clear view of the whole scene.

Without moving her head, her eyes dart over to me for a millisecond and then back to Arthur. Having seen firsthand how quickly he can move when not constantly monitored, I can understand her reluctance to look away.

"Shiv, do you still have his spectacles?" I ask, glancing over to the Ectoplasmic Containment Unit on the lobby desk.

She gives a little nod. Because of the missing fingers on her right hand, she holds the chair leg with the left. She reaches her mangled hand across her body and slips her thumb and pinky fingers into her vest pocket to retrieve the glasses. Her eyes hold their attention on Wilson the entire time, but her lips curl up in pain when her raw, oozing fingers drag against her body.

"I'm gonna have to toss 'em blind. Need you to do the leg work for the rest," she says, with the bridge of the spectacles pinched between her two remaining fingers.

"I'm ready."

Wilson lurches forward without warning, raising his bone saw to strike. The spectacles tumble out from the remnants of Shiv's hand, clattering across the floor toward the railing and coming to a stop with just the very edge of the lenses peeking over the edge. Shiv stumbles backward a few steps, raising the chair leg to block Arthur's attack. He swats it out of her hand easily, forcing a yip of surprised fear from her. Arthur raises the saw to strike again.

"Hey, four-eyes!" I shout to distract him, running up the stairs to join them on the balcony.

Arthur turns his head to me, his pearlescent eyes reflecting the light from the lobby chandelier. For once, I catch a sense of discontent on his face.

Ever since we got here, we've been nothing but mice, and he's been a cat batting us around. Now, there's a wrinkle in his plan. With me coming up from behind, he has to make a choice between finishing off his prey and protecting the last of the artifacts keeping his body invulnerable.

He only lets his guard down for a moment, but it invigorates me with a refreshed energy to finish this fight.

*****

Grab the spectacles. Turn to page 20.
Save Shiv. Turn to page 100.

Frankly, I have no idea which one is the right answer, and I've got a sinking feeling the wrong choice will end up with more of us dead. Rather than risk placing the incorrect thing in a bowl and having the room burst into flames, I see if there's a more creative solution.

"Everyone stand back." I grab one of the heftier jars off a shelf. It contains a severed human foot.

"Uh, Jeremy, what are you doing, bud?" PQ asks.

"I'm finding an alternate solution." I chuck the jar at the book's encasement, then turn my head away to protect my eyes from any splintering shards of glass. After the brief shattering symphony has passed, I take a look at my work to see if I've made any headway.

At first glance, it would seem I've managed to accomplish absolutely nothing, aside from dousing the case in a wet brine reeking of vinegar. Then I notice a small chip along the seam. "I think it's working. We just need to keep going."

PQ furrows his brow, looking a little disappointed. "Just so we're clear, then, our official plan is Hulk Smash?"

"Don't have to tell me twice." Shiv already has a brain in a jar slung over her shoulder and is getting ready to heave. She throws more aggressively, putting her whole body behind it. Her actions pay off, creating a spider web of cracks across the glass case.

"Nice throw!" I say, genuinely impressed by her strength and accuracy.

Shiv hoists another jar onto her shoulder, this one crammed with what I'm assuming are intestines. "One more alley-oop, and I think we should—"

"Stop right there!" A woman's voice instantly cuts off our plan.

During our cacophony of breaking jars, we didn't notice the door open behind us. Standing in its frame is Lucy, our host. She has a look of fury on her face, like an elementary school teacher who just caught some kids smoking in the bathroom. There is no fear in her, only indignant rage.

Shiv is so surprised, she drops her jar on the tile floor. It shatters, and pink-gray intestines unfurl with the speed of a snake getting ready to strike. All of our feet and ankles get splashed by formaldehyde.

"Do you people have no respect for private property? These are priceless heirlooms you're destroying here!"

"You bitch," I growl. "You killed Chrissy!"

"Technically, she allowed herself to die," Lucy says with just a hint of pettiness. "There were nearly a dozen viable pods in the morgue. To be honest, this is the first time we've had someone screw up so badly within the first five minutes. The burning morgue was literally meant to just light a fire under your asses. The fact that we lost a competitor that early means we'll have to go for more of a slow build next time. Don't get me wrong, it's good data, but my God, are you people dumb?"

I have a million questions for her but don't dare take a step forward, knowing any aggressive action will probably be met with twice as much retribution.

Shiv takes a different approach. She bursts into a sprint, tucking her head and heading straight into a tackle. Lucy steps back, revealing another woman behind her dressed in all black, with matching hair and bright red lipstick. The woman has a gun in her hand.

The muzzle flashes with a loud bang, and Shiv is on the floor, blood gushing out onto the white tile.

Lucy shakes her head, looking disappointed. "Such a shame. I was hoping to be able to just give you all a verbal warning, but it seems like we're going to have to call this whole round a wash. Charlotte, would you please?"

My eyes go wide when Charlotte trains her weapon on PQ. "No, wait," I say, but it's too late.

A single squeeze of the trigger, another flash, and one of PQ's eyes is missing. A spray of red hits the wall behind him.

Charlotte's got the gun pointed right at me. Searching for small favors, I figure with her crack-shot accuracy, at least she'll make it quick by shooting me in the—

*****

Try again. Turn to page 65.

We walk through a tinted glass door and step into a room covered in KMC Series posters ranging from reality trash, like *Holleywooed,* to their news program, *Realtime: True Facts.* A scrawny man with disheveled hair and an oversized suit sits at a desk in an otherwise empty waiting room lined with plastic chairs.

"Good morning," he says cheerfully. "Welcome to KMC Casting. My name is Todd. How can I help you today?"

"We have an appointment with Lucy Hodge."

Chrissy sounds casual while I'm totally geeking out about simply being on a studio lot. Even though we're in a seemingly normal-looking waiting room, it feels like more than that. It's a waiting room where movie magic is born.

Before Todd can respond, a blond woman with a black suit jacket and white turtleneck bursts through a side door. She has traces of baby fat on her face, despite being in her late thirties, and wears a look of hurried frustration. The woman makes it two steps before spotting us at the desk, upon which her demeanor completely shifts to one of a friendly tour guide. Her frowned red lips spread into a wide-open smile, revealing a set of perfect teeth. Her harsh brow softens.

"Hello! I'm Lucy Hodge, the host of the program you'll be testing today. You must be Chrissy and Jeremy."

We shake hands, then follow her through a hallway and into an elevator, where she presses a button for the third floor.

"Have you two tested game shows before?" Lucy asks as we rise.

"I've done a bunch of extra work, but this is my first game show."

"And are you two a couple?"

We both laugh.

"Just friends," I say. "We both go to film school together. I'm pretty sure she just brought me because she heard this was a puzzle-based game show and I'm good at that sort of stuff."

Lucy gives me an amused grin. "Well, you're half right. Come on, let's get some paperwork signed, and then I'll tell you all about it."

As if on cue, the elevator dings perfectly at the end of her sentence and opens into a busy office full of staff and cubicles. No matter where I look, I can't avoid seeing a giant KMC logo somewhere. Lucy leads us across the bullpen to a glass-walled office, where sitting on a table are two packets of paperwork.

"In front of you is a liability waiver, NDA, and questionnaire. Please be honest with your answers. This is a cutting-edge series we're testing here. Some of your answers will be vital in the information that we gather in order to put on the best show possible."

I sign the waiver after giving it a cursory glance. It's chock full of legalese I couldn't have deciphered even if I had read it carefully. I'm about to sign the NDA when I notice a clause that reads: "The participant shall not share any information about their activities or whereabouts for the duration of their lifetime."

"Wait, so I can't tell anyone about this *ever*? Even after the show comes out?" I ask.

Lucy nods. "That's right. If the series goes to air, you'll have knowledge of industry secrets that could compromise the technology behind the show. What happens during your play-test stays in your play-test."

*****

Sign the NDA. Turn to page 47.
Refuse to sign the NDA. Turn to page 33.

Upon re-reading the text, I remember the *Murder Mansion* movie about Wilson. There's this one scene that's endlessly ridiculed online and, even nearly a decade later, is still a meme I frequently see on Social. It's from the part of the film where Wilson—played by Landon Keating—finally confronts his father after he is caught in one of his hidden rooms, dissecting a victim.

In the scene, Arthur's father is understandably horrified and begs his son, "What are you doing?"

As a response, Arthur Wilson cranks his head at his father, eyes so wild they put Willem Dafoe to shame, then shouts, with a laughably unhinged delivery, "I'm doing science, goddammit!" He then proceeds to murder his own father, but that's neither here nor there, as far as this puzzle or meme are concerned.

"From what I remember about Arthur Wilson, it almost always comes down to science," I say. "Scientific improvement by any means was basically his life's only ambition, at least until he found the Amulet of Duriel and truly went mad."

"And how do you know that?" Shiv crosses her arms.

"I saw it in a meme once, when the movie came out."

"Just so we're all clear, you're making your choice purely based on the content of a meme that was popular, like, ten years ago, yeah?" Shiv asks.

My ears burn in embarrassment, partially because she has more or less hit the nail on the head. I make an effort to sound credible, cooking up an explanation that could be plausible. "In the journal entry, he talks about this Daniel kid but mostly as a control for a larger experiment. The black lung tests are the *point* of the diary entry. This priest he pickled is just the icing on top. I say we go with the escalating diseased samples."

Shiv gives me a skeptical look, though part of me thinks it's just because I didn't take her side. Still, she relents, and the three of us once again split up to look for dirty lungs with the appropriate test subjects' names on the labels. I find Bill Humber's moderately diseased lung in a jar that looks like it's filled with bile. Unlike the orange sponge that was Daniel's lung, this one is a sickly yellow, and it's covered in black spots.

"Still sure you want to be the scooper?" I ask PQ, showing him the jar.

"Was about to say the same thing." Shiv holds a jar containing what almost looks like several pieces of charcoal barely held together by little wisps of yellow tissue.

PQ does his best to hide a look of disgust upon seeing the diseased lungs, and I swear a small shudder passes through him. However, his voice carries a different tune. He speaks with what almost seems like too much enthusiasm.

"I mean, how many times does someone get an opportunity to hold diseased body parts from over a century ago?" He rubs his hands together and blows out a breath of air in preparation. "NDA or not, this is going in my memoir." He twists open the jar to Bill Humber's moderately diseased lungs, and our entire group holds our breaths this time to avoid the stench. PQ quickly dips his hand in the liquid and slides the blackened tissue under his palm. When he lifts it out, the sides droop, and a thinly hanging piece of tissue threatens to fall off.

"Gentle," Shiv commands, but PQ is already on it.

He scoops his other hand under the half-dissolved connective tissue and carefully places it into the second bowl.

Once again, we are encouraged by the middle lock rotating until its journey ends with a satisfying click. Shiv lets out a sigh of relief. Clearly, she did not believe in my theory that Wilson was more interested in the disease than humanity.

The first two jars smelled terrible, but this third one is so full of rancid, diseased meat that even though I'm holding my breath, I can taste death and chemicals when PQ pops the final lid. As soon as he dips a finger into the jar, a piece of the completely black lung drifts off from the whole. The black lung is so degraded, it's basically turned into the consistency of a wet paper towel that's been soaking overnight in water.

"I don't think I can fish this out," PQ says. "It's just going to disintegrate if I grab it."

We look around for some sort of ladle or tool that could help, but with the exception of the puzzle, table, and jars, there's not a single tool to be found in the room.

"All right." PQ rubs some sweat from his eyes and brow against his shoulder, making a point not to touch his face with his filthy hands. "Any ideas on how to transfer this last one to the bowl? You think maybe I can just, sort of...pour the whole thing in?"

I shake my head. "The bowl isn't big enough. It would be overflowing with liquid before the lungs even started to pour out." How I wish saying that hadn't just given me an idea. "Okay, PQ. I think I know what to do, but it's going to be a little...gross."

"Christ, just call me the goblin king of Grosstown already. What's the idea?"

I pick up the jar and fight back the urge to vomit. This one is by far the foulest smelling, so much so that Shiv has to retreat several steps. Even then, she can't help but make a gagging noise, threatening to push me over the edge and make me lose my lunch.

"All right," I say, after several breaths through my mouth, holding the jar as far from my face as possible. "Cup your hands and leave a little room between your fingers for the juice to leak through. Then you collect all the chunks of lung and drop them in the bowl."

PQ shakes his head and sighs. "Of all the things I expected for today, I never thought I'd become a human sieve for chunks of rotten lungs. Fine, let's get this over with so we can figure out whatever fresh hell comes next."

We both crouch close to the floor. PQ holds out his hands, forming a cup with a small hole between his pinky fingers. He then holds his arms out, avoiding as much splash-back onto his legs as possible. Slowly, I start to pour the contents of the jar into his hands.

"Hurrgghh," PQ gags.

"You okay?" I ask.

"Yeah, just starting to feel the chunks in my hand. So far, I give this hotel a zero out of ten. Do *not* recommend."

"Well, you're doing an awesome job," I say on reflex, too disgusted to even look at the jar I'm pouring into his hands.

Once it's empty, a pile of what could be black Jell-o wiggles in PQ's hands, and he carefully dumps it all into the third bowl.

At first, nothing happens.

My nerves are already on edge, throat constricted, holding down vomit. I'm on the verge of a panic attack, and my mind is racing. Did we somehow screw up the last bowl? Did I just make PQ go through all that for nothing?

Finally, there's the sound of a whizz-click at the bottom of the book's glass case and the sound of a larger metal mechanism releasing. I grab the rectangular glass lid. It lifts easily, revealing the book. When I pull it off the table, the door to the room creaks open of its own accord.

"Oh my God, it worked." I let out a heavy sigh of relief.

"Glad to see you were so confident in your plan," PQ says with just a hint of annoyance in his voice. He drags his hands against the wood table, trying to find any place other than his own clothes to clean them off.

I take a peek outside of the room to make sure there are no Banshees or ghostly serial killers in the hall. "I'd tell you to double-check the maps to be sure, but I think you're best off not touching anything until we can get you cleaned up. If I remember correctly, last time we looked at the map, there was something that looked like a staircase just to the left of this room."

I count my blessings that I'm now two for two. The staircase is just where I imagined it. Even better, the door is unlocked. After climbing a set of creaking wooden stairs, we step through another door and find ourselves in a carpeted hallway I recognize all too well from the big screen. The walls are covered in a maroon wallpaper, with gold fleur-de-lis in a pattern. Wall sconces provide a dim light, but after the basement, it's practically a night and day difference.

I look to my left, scream, and nearly jump out of my skin when I see a figure staring at me. It's only after I've made a total fool of myself I realize I'm looking at my own reflection in a floor-to-ceiling-length mirror with gold filigree.

"A little jumpy, are we?" Shiv pats me on the shoulder and casts a nonchalant glance in the mirror's direction.

"You're free to take the lead at *any* time," I say, soaking in the rest of my surroundings.

Directly across from the stairwell is a window peering into a two-chair barber shop, complete with a spinning red and white pole next to the door. Beside that is a shop just labeled "Provisions." A few steps further and we see a plain wooden door with a brass placard displaying the number "7."

"This must be one of the guest rooms." I casually try the handle and feel it turn easily in my hand. I look to PQ. "I'm sure there's a bathroom in here for you to wash up."

"Finally! I feel this is what Rudy Giuliani smells like after ten minutes in the sun. I'll be right back."

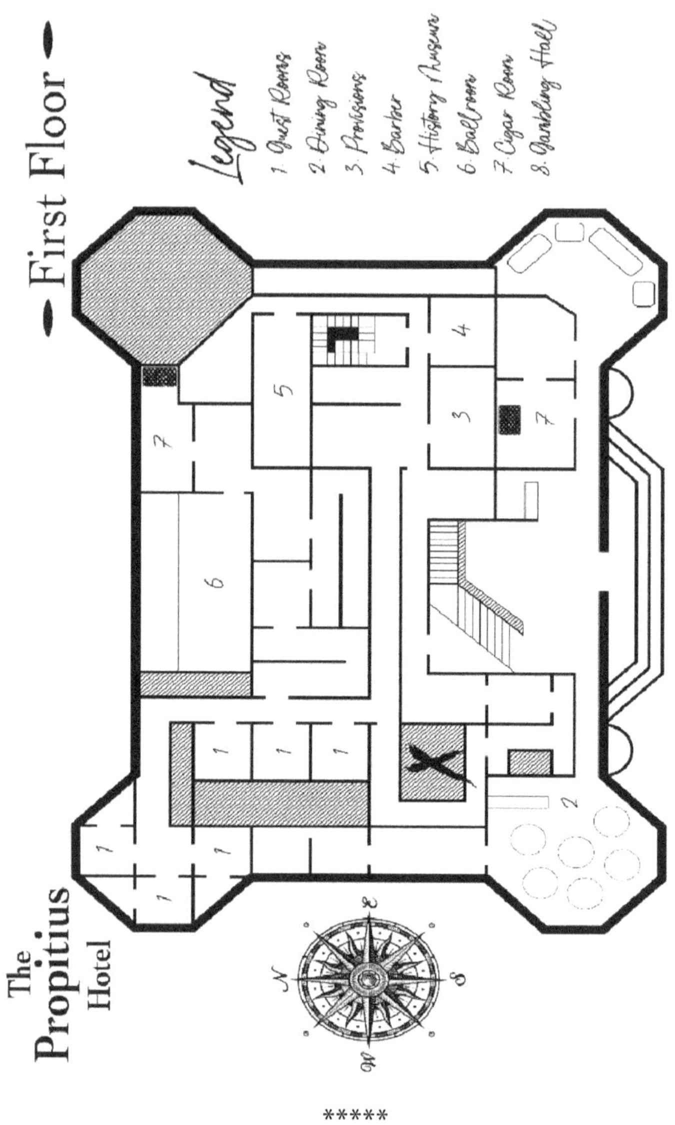

*****

Give PQ some privacy to clean up. Turn to page 117.
Try to keep everyone together. Turn to page 53.

I reach for the red-jeweled medallion hanging from his neck, seeing an opportunity to end this with one quick move. The chain snaps easily. Arthur is still in shock from his corporealization, so I reintroduce him to the world of physics with a hard knee to his balls. Real pain registers on his face, and he staggers back, hunched over. Even though he's tangible now, he's still dangerous. I chuck the amulet at the wall, but it barely leaves a dent in the gem. I bend over to pick it up and try again but realize that method probably won't cut it.

But I do know something that might...

I press Wilson's bone saw against the gem and saw at it feverishly.

Arthur regains his composure. He advances. I know I should move, but the saw's cutting through what turns out to be a gem made of hard plastic. In fact, the gold housing on the back is all plastic too, and the inside is hollow. If I can just hold on for a few more strokes, I'm sure I can cut the thing in half. That has to be enough to consider it destroyed, right?

There's no more joy in Wilson's face, only rage. He lunges at me just as I make one last cut, splitting the plastic amulet into two parts. Despite seeming like a cheap replica, a powerful blast of red energy sends both me and Wilson flying back. My head slams against the wall, and my spine cracks loudly.

I'm dizzy. My head throbs. I reach up and touch the back of my crown, my messy hair moist with blood. My back screams at me when I try to get up, but at least I can still move my arms and legs, so I know nothing is broken.

It hits me there's no reason to hurry getting up. The amulet has been destroyed, and somehow, I've managed to complete the game. So that begs the question, what do I do now?

No balloons are falling around me, no confetti flying from unseen corners. Also, no Krentler Media goons appearing from a hidden passage, with guns to finish me off.

I thought once this was over, I'd instantly be killed or released, but what if I was wrong about that? What if they just leave me here to die of starvation? A fresh wave of panic pushes through all my wounds and aching muscles, and I climb back to my feet, using the wall to keep my spinning head from booking me any return flights to the ground. It takes a few seconds and some deep breaths to get my head on straight enough to realize why no one has been sent to fetch me yet.

It's not over.

Like a serial killer from some slasher movie, Arthur Wilson sits up. He stares at me with laser focus, opens his coat, and produces a large nail from his pocket—might as well be a railroad spike. It's followed by a medical equivalent of a ball-peen hammer. I have no idea how he's able to keep so many weapons tucked in such small pockets, but that's the least of my worries right now. I'm still trying to figure out how he's still alive. I destroyed the amulet. Wasn't that the assignment?

I put up my arms to defend myself, but I'm so weak, I'm little more than a marionette to him. He presses my exhausted arm against the wall and places the tip of the nail in the center of my palm.

"Please, wait," I say, knowing full well it will have no effect on what's about to happen.

He drives the hammer into the nail, and the world flashes white with pain for a moment. This happens three more times, Arthur impaling the spike deeper into the wall. Once he's satisfied, he grabs my other arm and holds it out, repeating the process with a new nail he pulls from inside of his sleeve. Now that he's in human form, I can feel his cold hand press into my wrist when he aligns the second nail. The second one doesn't hurt as bad, but I'm lightheaded, like I'm about to pass out.

Just as the world goes dark, a hand grabs my hair and pulls my head up to face Arthur's. There's a sickly sweet tang on his hot breath. He tries out his new voice box.

"Don't worry," he says. "I'll be here when you wake up. I've got all sorts of treats for you."

*****

The correct answer was to go for the throat.
Turn to page 138.

"I know this is going to sound crazy, but I think we should split up."

Shiv looks like she might put an end to me before Arthur even finishes making it up the stairs. "I'm sorry, but that sounds like a terrible idea."

I nod. "It is, but I can't think of a better one right now. This house is a maze. If we split up, maybe one of us can find another way down, or at least clear a path down this main stairway into the lobby."

Shiv stares suspiciously at me. "And of course, the person you're referring to is you, as *you* have the spectacles. If we split up and you get offed by Arthur, what the hell am I supposed to do?"

I glance back at the stairs. Arthur is taking his time climbing each one, as if he were an '80s slasher who only ever walked yet always seemed to catch up to the sprinting victim. Still, we've got to hurry and make a decision.

"Fine," I say, pulling the glasses from my pocket and thrusting them toward Shiv. "You take the glasses. I'll be the distraction. Just meet me back in the lobby as soon as you can."

Shiv's face registers genuine confusion. Now that she's been entrusted with the key to our potential survival, she doesn't look so tough anymore. She looks lost...and afraid.

"You can do this. Just keep moving, try not to get cornered, and any time the light flickers, haul ass."

We both start backing up into the hallway when Arthur reaches the top of the stairs.

"Are we seriously doing this?" Shiv asks.

I nod, though I can't tell if she's looking at me. Instead, I'm weighing options at the end of the hallway. "If I remember the map right, I think there's more places to navigate if you make a left at the end of the hall. It'll give you more options. I'll go right."

Shiv sucks in a breath of air through her mouth as if she's about to say something. Whether it's going to be an insult or a compliment is anyone's guess. Her eyes dart back toward our assailant, and she pats me on the shoulder before breaking into a sprint. I don't hesitate to join her down the long corridor. We hit a T-intersection, and she turns left, as planned. I pause, buying her a few seconds and letting Arthur set his sights on me.

As Shiv runs, she calls out, "Don't die!"

Arthur calmly stalks toward me in his brown tweed suit. From this distance, his mouth is obscured by his bushy mustache, but I can almost guarantee he's smiling. The bill of his hat shrouds most of his face in darkness, save for two gleaming dots for eyes.

I consider taunting him, to further set his sights on me, but I can already feel my knees trembling and my ankle throb. There's no need to add insult to my potential injury. I glance to the side to see if Shiv is still in the hall.

She's gone.

The wall sconces flicker, and in the blink of an eye, Arthur has advanced upon me by nearly twenty feet, his suit replaced by a bloodstained surgeon's apron. His hat has been switched with a white cotton cap, and his mouth is obscured by a mask. Instead of brandishing the hacksaw, he now holds up a tiny scalpel, which for some reason seems even more frightening.

I've bought Shiv enough time. I need to get the hell out of here. To my left is a room with a bronze placard labeled "Cigar Room." In front of me is an archway leading deeper into the hotel, and to my right is another long hall basically making a U-turn from the previous hall I just came from.

*****

Enter the door on the left. Turn to page 133.

Go straight. Turn to page 136.
Make another immediate right. Turn to page 125.

I have no idea what a Bean Sidhe is, but Shiv's scaring me. "What *is* that?" I ask.

"You'd call it a Banshee in America. The weeping woman. Just leave her be."

I want to ask her how she knows what this thing is and what the hell it's doing down here. Instead, I decide now's not really the time for a conversation and just let her lead. "Okay. What should we do?"

"Get as far as we can from her and pray she doesn't see us." Shiv reaches the door but hesitates to cross. "Is she gone?"

I peer outside again. No, I can't see her, even though her wail is just as loud as it was before. "I think the coast is clear," I say.

"Good." Shiv takes off without warning, making a halfhearted attempt at moving quietly. She bolts in the opposite direction of the crying specter.

PQ and I both follow, though I'm not sure he and I are doing any better of a job at being stealthy. We come to the end of a hall, where we reach a T-junction.

"Which way?" I ask, as if any of us could possibly have the answer.

"I could check the map," PQ offers, reaching for his back pocket.

"Screw that. We're going right. I can feel it in my gut." Shiv takes off running, losing the pretense of trying to be sneaky.

We follow until the pervading wail turns into an ear-piercing scream. It's so loud it trips PQ up in his tracks. He knocks into me, and we fall. My top priority, even as I'm crashing to the floor, is covering my ears.

The scream eventually subsides, and I force a yawn to pop my eardrums. I'm shocked back to reality when a hand grips me by the forearm.

It's Shiv.

"We have to go *now*."

She practically pulls the two of us to our feet, and we all take off stumbling down the hall. We come to another intersection, and Shiv leads with another right. She doesn't make it more than a few steps before her momentum gets completely halted, smashing into a black mass standing just around the bend.

The Banshee holds out a hand, each finger starting as pale as a corpse and slowly turning to blackened rot, ending in a sharpened nail longer than any human's I've seen. Two of the Banshee's nails are poked right into Shiv's eyes. My companion stutters something, and her arms twitch. Blood runs a stark contrast against her skin and trickles down her face. Her legs can only hold her so long, and she falls to the floor, leaving PQ and me face-to-face with a creature sporting bloodshot eyes and a gaping chasm of a mouth.

"Oh crap," PQ says, slowly backing away.

The Banshee's attention shifts to him for a moment, but then moves to me. I'm frozen in place, transfixed in horror by her bright red eyes. In a flash, she's on top of me. I can't move my arms or legs. Worse, I can't catch my breath.

With a hand, she places a bloody rag over my face, and suddenly, it feels like all the nerves in my body are being ripped up and out of my lungs. I'm not just in pain; I'm being consumed. Every piece of my essence is getting sucked out from inside of me. There's a tremendous pressure on my chest. Something cracks, and what feels like a dozen internal knives impale all my vital organs.

*****

The correct answer was to investigate the sound.
Turn to page 76.

Despite what my lizard brain is telling me, I have to use every ounce of willpower to back off and let Todd go. There are a lot of things I'm willing to do to escape, but I would never resort to murder.

At least, that's what I *want* to believe.

"The lobby," I say, staring Todd in the eyes. "What's the fastest way there?"

"Down the ladder, through the door that says: 'History Museum.' Please don't kill me," he begs, tears and snot running down his face.

I give him my best impression of Shiv's resting mean-girl face, then hurry down the ladder. The room-between-rooms I land in is similar to the one above. It takes a minute to find the panel with black gaff tape over it, the words "History Museum" scribbled in silver sharpie.

I crawl through the door and find myself in a large room full of glass-encased display cabinets, with pictures and maps all over the walls. On the left wall is a large model house. At first, I assume it's a model of The Propitius, but it's not. It's a house I haven't seen in over a decade—my childhood home. The room is dark, save for one spot. The only light source comes from a second-floor window of the model house, which glows a constantly shifting orange and red.

My bedroom.

Brian's bedroom.

My fingers glide across the displays. I'm drawn toward the house, and all the items inside the glass are things I recognize. Brian's first stuffed animal, a brown dog named Woofie. He'd taken scissors and cut off half the hair on the stuffed animal's face because he had been worried Woofie's hair would get in his eyes and make it hard for him to see. Another display features assorted pages of a comic book Brian and I made together—*The Adventures of Morpho Man*. We spent weeks drawing this single issue about a hero who looked suspiciously like Wolverine and had the ability to transform into anything, but mostly chose to become a motorcycle.

"Keep going," Brian says behind me.

I don't turn around, knowing whatever form he's taken is likely custom-tailored to reignite as much trauma in me as possible. Instead, I do as he says, passing by several other relics of our childhood—all lost in the fire—and approach the model house. Bending over slightly, I peek through the window and see the worst moment of my life played out.

Inside, two tiny toys come to life. The boy whose bed is pressed against the window sits up, frozen in fear, while the boy on the opposite side of the bedroom screams, trapped in a blazing inferno. The heater, located in the attic, had short-circuited and caused a fire, which didn't spread to the rest of the house until it had burned its way through the attic floor. Sitting between the two brothers sits a blazing ceiling beam, collapsed under the weight of the heater.

I turn away, knowing what happens next, but as I do, I'm no longer in the museum. I'm in my bed, and my room is on fire.

"Jeremy, help!" little six-year-old Brian shouts from his bed, which looks like it's being swallowed by hell itself.

I shake my head, tears falling from my cheeks. I know what's expected of me now, how the house wants me to react. But I won't let it. In its attempt to bring me back to that place of guilt and crippling shame that's followed me my entire life, it ended up doing the opposite.

"Help me!" Brian shouts again, this time with even more urgency. He reaches out a hand, and his SpongeBob-pajama-covered arm bursts into flames.

"I couldn't. There's no way I could have done anything in this situation as an eight-year-old, never mind an adult. I'm sorry, Brian. I love you, and I've missed you every day of my life, but I realize now that there was nothing I could have done to save you."

I turn to the window, just like I did as a child, and climb out. Instead of stepping onto a gray-tiled roof, I'm back inside the museum. Brian is standing in front of me, looking more horrifying than even in my worst nightmares. His face is melted, his hair gone. Black charred flakes of his pajamas are cooked onto his sagging skin. His fingers are webbed from the heat fusing them together. I squeeze my hands into fists and fight back the urge to fall apart.

"Brian, I can't help you."

"Jeremy, I need you. Please!" he cries, holding out a tiny malformed hand.

My breath comes in shudders. I want to reach out to him, to hold him one last time. But there's nothing I can do to change the past.

"I'm sorry this happened to you, but I need to go." I hold back a dam of emotion. "I have to live my life."

A smoldering flame around Brian's feet catches, and his legs slowly melt into the circle of fire. He makes one final attempt, screaming and crying so loudly it makes my whole body shiver.

"Jeremy, don't leave me! He stole me away from the happy place and won't stop hurting me. If you go away now, he'll have me trapped in this house forever. You *have* to help me!"

Panic rises in me as he drips into the floor, getting smaller by the second. What if what he's saying is true? Could Arthur Wilson and his amulet have dragged my brother's spirit from some peaceful afterlife into this house? Can the dead even *be* hurt?

Then it hits me. The house wasn't trying to fool me with the fire. It knew I wouldn't fall for conjured old memories.

This is the real game.

I've let my brother down once, and as soon as I've forgiven myself of that guilt, it's now forcing me straight into another choice—one I may never actually learn the truth about. I could push on, reigniting the guilt and shame that's followed me all these years, living in constant doubt whether I did the right thing or, once again, doomed my brother. Or I can make up for a decade of survivor's guilt and see things through with Brian, wherever they may lead us.

*****

Leave Brian. Turn to page 153.
Join Brian. Turn to page 99.

Leave Brian. Turn to page 153.
Join Brian. Turn to page 99.

Throughout this entire process, Lucy hasn't given me a single reason to believe she's even remotely telling the truth. Of course, this is still part of the game. Until I'm either at home, in my bed, or buried six feet deep, the game will never be over.

I get up out of the barber's chair and stumble across the room toward Lucy's table.

"Careful now," she says.

My spider-bitten ankle rolls on uneven ground, causing me to hiss out a curse and nearly fall.

"We have a medical team on standby, ready to address all of your wounds just as soon as we're done here. First question. You had previous relationships with several of your fellow companions. Did you find that helped or hurt your experience in the game?"

I open my mouth, confident of my answer at first, but stop myself before committing. Of course, having pre-existing relationships helped me. Without their support, I would have felt so much more alone throughout this process. But then I think better of it and shake my head.

"No. It makes it so much harder to lose people I care about. I would have preferred strangers."

"Hmm." Lucy types something on a tablet she brings up from her lap. "In our tests with total strangers, we found it very hard to weave a compelling narrative. I think more research is required there. Question two. How did you feel about the amulet's manifestation of your fear? Did you find it to be comparable to the manifestations of your partners'?"

I shake my head. "Not at all. You forced me to be haunted by my dead brother, tried to get him to push me over the edge with the guilt I already felt. I cannot stress enough how cruel that was. Meanwhile, all you had for PQ were some spiders?"

"So, you felt PQ's fear wasn't substantial enough?"

I feel like this is a trick question and there's no right answer. I also feel just a little guilty for trivializing what must have been a very real fear for PQ. It seems disrespectful to speak about my dead friend in that way. "I just think it was different."

Lucy narrows her eyes and studies my face, trying to read me. "I agree," she says, finally breaking eye contact and re-focusing on typing notes onto her tablet. "I think personal trauma is much stronger than a surface-level fear, both for entertainment value and character development."

Hearing Lucy refer to my dead brother as "entertainment value" forces me to bite my lip and clench my fists. I fight the urge to break the champagne flute in front of me and stab it into Lucy's eye.

"Okay, one final question, and this one's for all the marbles. I'll preface by already letting you know you made the smart choice in choosing to sit here and talk with me, and in return, I'm ready to offer you something. Obviously, we can't let you leave here. While everything we said before about NDAs is true, we can't risk even a whisper of this getting out before we're ready for the premiere. So, here's the deal. I already saw in your application that you're about to graduate from film school. Is that right?"

I nod, dreading where this is going.

"Well, as I'm sure you're aware by now, we're putting together a reality series unlike anything that's ever been attempted before. And in order to pull it off, we're going to need a proper crew." Lucy taps a few buttons on her tablet, then brings up a contract, which she sets in front of me. "Feel free to take your time to read over it, but the long-short of it is that you will stay here in town, starting today, as a full-time employee of Krentler Media. You will work on the production of *Slashtag* until the program has aired, at which point you will be transferred to a senior position at our production office. What do you want to be? A director? Writer? Producer? Actor? We are ready to make your filmmaker dreams come true, and all you have to do is sign on the dotted line."

I grab the tablet and scroll quickly over ninety-six pages of legalese, to a final page where my name, Jeremy Talbott, is printed just below a line where I'm prompted to sign.

This is my final choice of the day, and it's arguably the biggest one of all. But when it really comes down to it, I don't really have a choice at all, do I?

THE END

We hope you enjoyed the interactive adventure and are
ready for some more fun.
If you haven't read it yet, check out *Slashtag*.

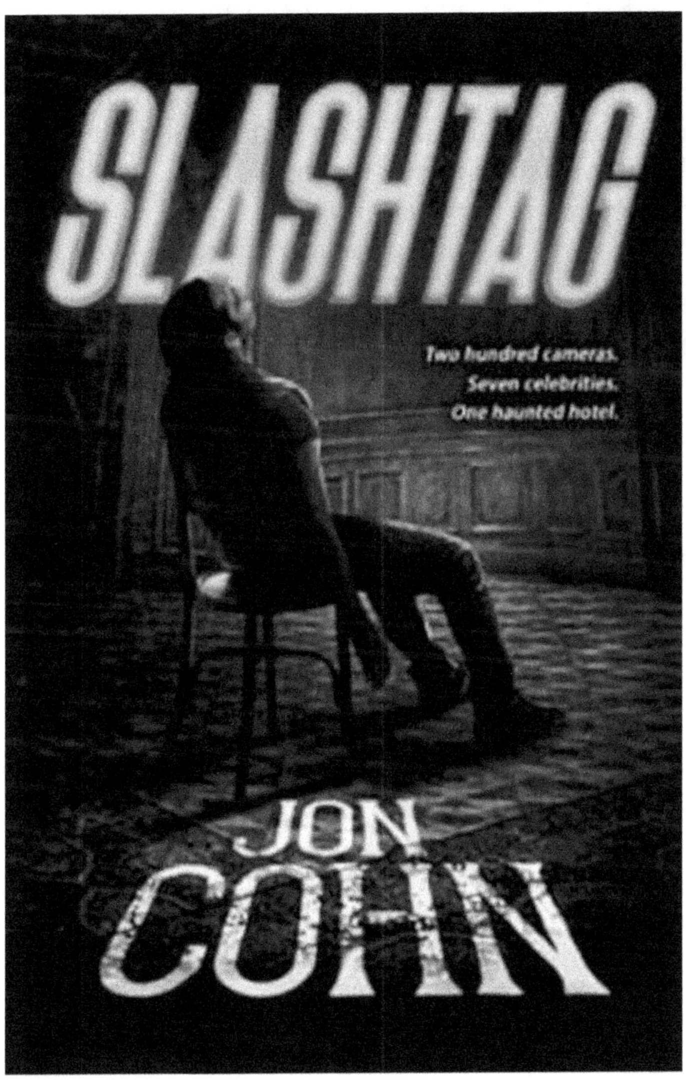

Step Into the Grind House

Pre-order Grind House 2.0– the horror party board game for 2-8 brave souls, designed by Jon Cohn. This bloodsoaked board game is set within the *Slashtag* universe, complete with a dedicated Propitius Hotel Expansion! You may have survived Arthur Wilson, now try your luck against The Host as he takes you on a tour of the Grind House. If you're lucky, admission will only cost an arm and a leg.

Coming Summer 2024.

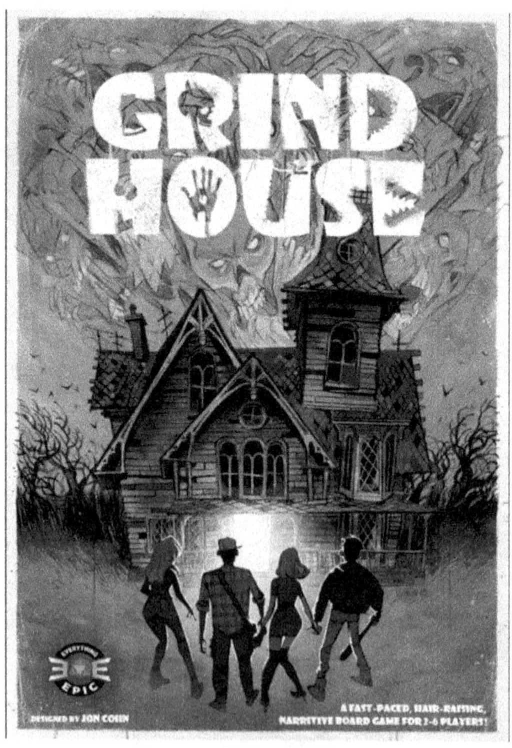

Visit Everything Epic to see this and other great games.

Other Books by Jon Cohn

The Island Mother

Slashtag

Everything is Temporary

Coming 2025 from Wicked House Publishing: *The Creed Falls Massacres*

Visit www.joncohnauthor.com for more.

Download Your Free Copy

Includes the first two chapters and one death scene from each of the first seven books in the Try Not to Die series.

Jon Cohn is one of the talented authors in the
Dethfest Confessions anthology.
Look for his story "Fight Fire With Fire."

Time for a Decision

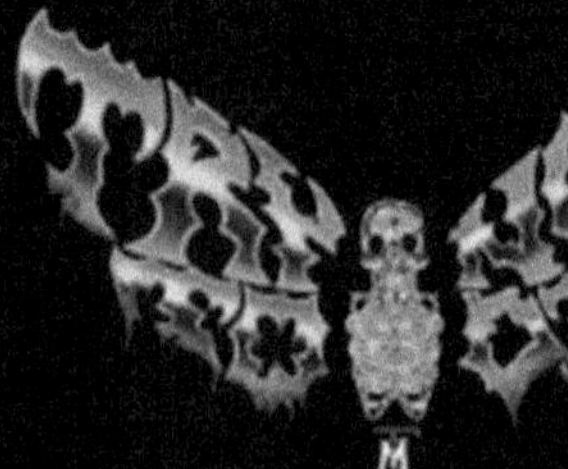

Which books do you want to die in?

Coming Soon

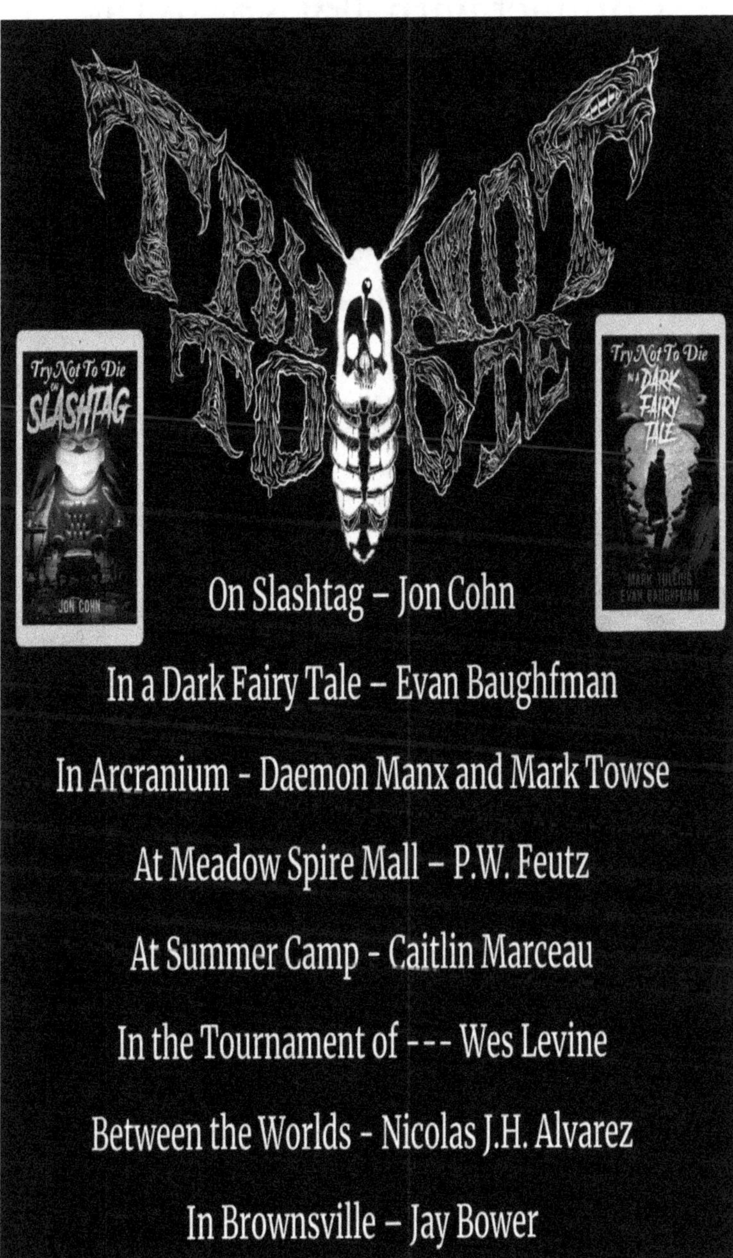

On Slashtag – Jon Cohn

In a Dark Fairy Tale – Evan Baughfman

In Arcranium - Daemon Manx and Mark Towse

At Meadow Spire Mall – P.W. Feutz

At Summer Camp - Caitlin Marceau

In the Tournament of --- Wes Levine

Between the Worlds - Nicolas J.H. Alvarez

In Brownsville – Jay Bower

Connect with Try Not to Die

The Try Not to Die series has its own social media pages. Check them out on IG at

https://geni.us/TryNotToDieOnIG

In addition to Instagram, you can also check them out on Tik Tok at

https://geni.us/TryNotToDieOnTikTok

And on Facebook find the series at

https://geni.us/TryNotToDieOnFacebook

Your Free Book is Waiting

Get a free copy of this collection
Morsels of Mayhem: An Unsettling Appetizer here:
MarkTullius.com